Voices
Rising

Voices Rising

Native Women Writers

Teresa Peterson
Tashia Hart
Gabrielle Tateyuskanskan
Annastacia Cardon
Evelyn Bellanger
Rosetta Peters
Janice Bad Moccasin
Zibiquah Denny

Edited by
Diane Wilson
Zibiquah Denny

Voices Rising: Native Women Writers

ISBN: 978-1-7369493-9-9

Editors: Diane Wilson
                                    Zibiquah Denny
Cover Art: Tashia Hart
Back Cover Group Photo: Ne-Dah-Ness Greene
Book Design & Typesetting: Paul Nylander, Illustrada Design

Published by
Black Bears & Blueberries Publishing
www.blackbearsandblueberries.com

Publication Date: July 2021

Printed and bound in the United States of America

*Dedicated to the ancestors who left us with strength,
resilience and stories.*

Table of Contents

Introduction
      Diane Wilson. 1

Voices from Pejuhutazizi: Dakota Stories and Storytellers
      Teresa Peterson. 3

Native Love Jams
      Tashia Hart 13

Ista Wicayaza Wi *"The Moon of Snow Blindness"*
      Gabrielle Tateyuskanskan. 23

King to Be
      Annastacia Cardon. 33

Mewinzha
      Evelyn Bellanger 43

The Spider and The Rose
      Rosetta Peters 53

The Sacred Road Trip
      Janice Bad Moccasin. 65

Naming Ceremony
      Zibiquah Denny 75

Contributors 85

Acknowledgements 91

Introduction

In June 2020, while we were all still reeling from the aftermath of George Floyd's death, and in the midst of a pandemic, we launched the Native Authors Program as a project of All My Relations Arts. The program was a response to the underrepresentation of Native authors and books in publishing as well as in literary grants and awards. The Native Authors Program was formed to support emerging Native writers in completing a book-length manuscript for publication.

But the true goal of the program was far more ambitious: we wanted to ensure that Native stories and histories would be written by Native authors. We wanted our children and future generations to have books that were told from an indigenous perspective, rather than the whitewashed narrative that many of us learned in public school. Both All My Relations Arts and the Franklin branch of the Hennepin County Library have supported this goal from the beginning. I am especially grateful to Angela Two Stars and Becky Wolf for their vision and encouragement.

The Native Authors Program builds on the work of many dedicated Native writers and teachers who have supported similar work over the years and offered their wisdom in the planning stages. In this pilot year, we were blessed to work with visiting guest writers: Heid Erdrich, Kimberly Blaeser, Thomas Peacock, Marcie Rendon and Rebecca Roanhorse. Thomas Peacock and Betsy Albert-Peacock

(Black Bears and Blueberries Publishing), have generously contributed their time and expertise in helping to publish this anthology.

Much gratitude goes to the panel of editors who offered their insights into the publishing process: Gordon Henry, (Michigan State University Press), Joey McGarvey (Milkweed Editions), Erik Anderson, (University of Minnesota Press), and Ann Regan (MN Historical Society Press). And finally, our thanks to arts funders Sherrie Fernandez-Williams (MSAB) and Eleanor Savage (Jerome Foundation) for their encouragement and support.

Most of all, I want to thank the eight writers who accepted the invitation to be part of this first cohort, and committed their time and energy to working on manuscripts over the past year. For any writer, that means carving out time in a busy life, allowing ourselves to be vulnerable, and committing to the long discipline of writing a book. For Native writers, that can also mean pushing through the layers of trauma that are often part of our stories.

It has been my great pleasure and honor to serve as the Mentor for this group in the past year. I could not be more proud of the ways ·in which each writer has stepped up to challenge themselves to share their stories, develop their writing craft, and work towards completing their books. The heartfelt and imagined stories you'll read in this collection remind us how beautifully diverse and creative we are as indigenous people, as we share our humor, our truths, our sorrows, and our visions for the future.

Mitakuye Owasin,

Diane Wilson
2020–2021 Mentor
Native Authors Program

Voices from Pejuhutazizi: Dakota Stories and Storytellers

Teresa Peterson

This excerpt is taken from the first section in the soon to be released book, Voices from Pejuhutazizi: Dakota Stories and Storytellers *(Minnesota Historical Society Press, November 1, 2021). The book is a collection of Dakota stories across five generations from Pejuhutazizi K'api, the place where they dig the yellow medicine told by my uncle Was'icunhdinaz'in, Walter LaBatte Jr and my great grandfather Wanbdiska, Fred Pearsall. Utuhu Cistinna Win emakiyapi ye, they call me Little Oak.*

INTRODUCTION

Francis tipped his cowboy hat back, looked at me and said, "Your tree has no roots." I replied with silence and a blank stare. I looked down at my wispy, blowing-in-the-wind tree drawn on the stark white 11" x 13" paper. "You're searching for something," he declared.

This time I responded with a bewildered, "What? What am I looking for?"

"That's for you to figure out," he replied.

And that was that. My *tree-reading* was over. With nothing more to say, I shook his hand and thanked him. No epiphanies, no *aha Oprah* moments. The thoughts briefly wafted in my mind on the drive home, knowing it was significant but frustrated with my apparent lack of tree interpretation.

That was the spring of 2000. I was a wife and mother of two- and four-year old boys and working as a post-secondary counselor at a charter school serving predominantly Native students. We began our days with smudging with the students circled around the drum singing the Dakota Flag Song. This cultural grounding happened before we moved into the academic routine. Our days were rooted in Dakota worldview coupled with experiential learning and traditional book learning. The small base of students and staff allowed us the flexibility to participate in community events, workshops, and con-ferences - those often filled by adults. It offered relevant and engaging educational experiences not often found in textbooks. We learned together, students and staff. One such community event included a two-day Red Road Gathering, and it was during the second day of the workshop, with very little instruction, we were each asked to draw a tree. I had anxiously awaited my turn for a *tree reading* and wondered what could possibly be gleaned from my dismally drawn and uninter-esting tree.

At the time, I did not understand what any of this meant, but it stuck with me over the years. It has taken me all this time to return to this place, now with more understanding. I was then in essence, a tree with no roots. What I had understood and learned of my culture up to this point provided a foundation to my Dakota identity. And yet in hindsight, I was missing so much more. I once heard that knowing who you are, has every bit to do with knowing whose you are. How does one come to understand who you belong to? Dakota ia, Utuhu Can Cistinna emakiyapi ye—*in Dakota,* **they** *call me Little Oak Tree.* I am the granddaughter of many . . . many of whom brought me here to this place in time.

From our past to the present, I now realize that it is stories that carry us into our collective future. Many of the stories in this collec-tion are of resiliency and strength, courage and fortitude. My ances-tor's stories remind me, I am meant to be here—not by chance but for purpose. What I have come to understand is that we all have story.

Our story is part of shaping our sense of belonging and place in the world. When we know our story, we belong no matter where we go, where we are.

Dakota Stories. Within our community, there are two types of stories. Wicoooyake stories include history, migration, and genealogy of the people. Hitunkakanpi stories include tales, legends, and myths. Both types of stories do more than entertain. They enlarge the mind and stimulate imagination. Stories convey the values of the people and pass on traditions. Stories remind us of our heroes and the feats they have accomplished. Stories have a way of conveying what is sometimes so difficult to grasp, ushering in much needed clarity and understanding. Sometimes stories reconcile the past, making things right. Stories tell of place and provide the roots that connect people to land. Stories can illustrate how spirit exists in all things through both literal and symbolic truths and metaphors. They also provide entertainment, connecting storyteller and listener. Stories remind us of who we are, where we come from, and provide us direction. They shape identity, values, and ways of being. Stories connect us to the future, and for those of the next generation—a connection to the past. Today, hitunkakanpi and wicoooyake stories are sometimes kept alive through rare written accounts, yet some Dakota families and communities continue to rely upon the oral traditions of gifted storytellers.

The Storytellers. Ella Deloria, a Dakota linguist, ethnographer, and writer from the early 1900s explained that there were Dakota storytellers that could recount three hundred winter counts all from memory and without error. Storytelling is a gift, and love and respect are gained by the storyteller. The role of the storyteller is to preserve history and legend, pass on traditions and values, connect listeners to people and place, and entertain. The primary storytellers in this collection are my great grandpa Wanbdiska aka Fred Pearsall and my uncle, Was'icunhdinaz'in aka Walter 'Super' LaBatte Jr.

Wanbdiska shares Dakota stories from long ago, including those he heard from his mother-in-law, Tasinasusbecawin, my great-great-grandmother. Grandpa Fred intended on publishing his stories but did not live long enough to realize his goal. In 1983, his daughter Wanske, aka Cerisse Pearsall Ingebritson, self-published a book of his stories, titled 'Stories and History of Dakota People (Sioux) by Fred Pearsall'. Cerisse shared that she 'did it partly for those who still remember her father . . . but the book holds much for those much younger as well.' Mom gave me her copy when I left for college, both of us not really realizing the importance of it at the time. The book is long out of print, bringing my copy, now tattered and held together with a rubber band, a treasured family heirloom.

Several years ago, I was able to ask Cerisse about the book while visiting her and taking advantage of her sunny home in Phoenix. She was my grandma Genevieve's older sister—my great aunt. In the Dakota way, she would have just been my grandma. During these visits, I learned more about her and her sisters' early lives. She described how she and my grandma had to hook up the horses and wagon to travel. She shared that she and grandma were the first Indians to go to the public school in town. I laugh now as she disclosed, I don't know how Gen graduated because she never studied. While the sisters remained close, their demeanor and lifestyles seemed completely different. Cerisse lived a more prim and refined life, my grandma more common and comforting, much like my own mother. I appreciate both. Cerisse introduced me to new ideas, like Native art. She shared story of having kept a friendship with R.C. Gorman and supported other artists with purchases of their baskets, beadwork, and paintings. I can still hear her fondness for the baskets displayed on her wall, 'I think they make your house homey.' In between visits, we shared letters. She shared words of encouragement for pursuing college and career that I imagine resonated with her own independent life. She kept me updated of the neighbors who checked in on her and of 'Homeless' the cat she fostered. Eventually, we decided I would rewrite her book so that others might enjoy her father's writings. I am reminded of that promise as I walk from room to room of my home—a signed art card by Gorman to Cerise hangs on my office wall, her baskets displayed in the living room making it feel homey, and a large oil painting from another artist centered in my dining room. She died late summer in 2011, two weeks before her 101st birthday, long before I would fulfill my commitment.

Grandpa Fred's stories from Cerisse's book are now joined by my uncle's stories to form a collection of stories. Deksi (Uncle) Super shares stories of his memories and those he heard growing up in Pejuhutazizi. From time to time, I would hear him tell stories when he was giving a talk for a group, or some formal presentation I had wheedled him into. Sometimes Deksi would tell a story for me to figure out—a solution to a seeming dilemma, never explicitly giving me an answer. On these occasions it might take me days to figure out what teaching the story had to offer. More recently, my uncle has found a captivated audience through Facebook to share his stories. Recognizing his gift of stories and storytelling, I asked Deksi to join me in completing this book project. Together, we have had to figure out an amicable route for the book, with differing motivations, voices, and perspectives. More importantly, we both agree stories are meant to be shared and passed from one generation to the next.

Coming Together. This book project has taken detours, gotten lost, found new roads, and has evolved into a broader collection of stories from Wanbdiska, Was'icunhdinaz'in, and voices from Pejuhutazizi. As the narrator, you will also hear a part of my story. Our book, *Voices from Pejuhutazizi: Dakota Stories and Storytellers* is organized into four parts. Part One answers the question, *Why are these stories important to me?* Part Two shares introductory information of primary story characters and the intergenerational and relational connections that span between them. Part Three is the collection of stories from Wanbdiska and Was'icunhdinaz'in. The stories are organized thematically and offer intersections across generations.

> **Stories impart values:** teaching us how to live and behave from one generation to the next.
> **Stories transmit traditions**: passing on cultural practices that give tribute and honor to unique ways of being and doing.

Stories deliver heroes: inspiring us through the actions of others, especially those we have not read in school or can find in history books.

Stories reconcile: offering understanding and opportunity to make things right.

Stories entertain: bringing delight to listeners.

Stories of place: reminding and connecting us to this land we call home.

Stories provide belonging: nurturing kinship, community, and connectedness.

Part Four answers the question, *How have these stories changed me?* While each voice is distinct, the storytellers are differentiated by typeface. Brief and limited annotation is included, and a glossary is provided for translations of Dakota words that are not defined in text.

I encourage you as you read through the collection of stories, just as I have, to discover the teachings within each and identify links to your own personal story. As you make connections with the stories and storytellers, you might recognize how in some ways we are all the same—and yet different. This is the power of stories—the ability to cultivate our shared humanity because truly, we all have a story.

PART I: WHY ARE THESE STORIES IMPORTANT TO ME?

I have been working on this writing project for many years and it has transformed several times over. All the while I knew and felt in my heart that these stories were important and without a doubt changed me. But it was not until I was part of a Native women's writing group that my own story became part of the story. My group asked me quite frankly, 'Why are these stories important to you?' They encouraged me to dig deep to answer the question and tell of the stories' impact on me. They believed it was an integral piece to this work and that many would be able to relate to. And so, I answer that simple yet loaded question by sharing a bit of my own story.

It was a summer over the fourth of July that we took a visit to one of my husband's relatives in the Peever area over on the Lake Traverse

Reservation. This was a few years back, when our boys were young, and they loved running around with their tahansis (male cousins). It was the home of one of his 'uncles', a relative of his grandma's that I had not yet met. After a meal, visiting, and watching fireworks, we got up to head back to our motel and I proceeded to shake everyone's hands. As I was going down the line of lawn chairs, I heard his uncle ask a younger relative next to him, 'Who was that? See how she is. That's because she knows who she is.' It was by that time in my life I had learned enough of my family's story, gained enough confidence in my own identity, that I understood—when you know yourself, no matter where you go, you belong.

I have come to understand that stories are integral in shaping our cultural identities. Damakota (I am Dakota). It is through these stories I have a better understanding of what that means—what it means to be a Dakota winyan (woman). I think a part of it is knowing who you are, who you belong to - and it is that understanding that is most often gained through stories. Sure, I was raised in relationship to my mother's family—my grandma, my aunties and cousins, and the like. But it was not until later in my life that I learned of our stories of long ago, our history told through story, stories of place, and stories of relatives and their resilience and strength. Stories of my great great-grandmother whose life and legacy brought forward a daughter, five granddaughters, and ultimately me to this place and time that has become now part of my story.

When I think about my own story, I immediately reflect on my bicultural identity. I am Dakota and White (German). I was not raised in my mother's home at Pejuhutazizi with the comfort of Dakota relatives constantly nearby. To the contrary, mainstream society—the white society enveloped me. It was everywhere in my childhood—school, media, neighbors, friends, and church. Yet, I inherently knew I was 'Indian' and that I was different than my surroundings. But what did it mean to be 'Indian' or 'Sioux'? Other than my mom telling me to 'marry Indian', I do not remember anyone explaining to me what that meant or sharing stories about our Dakota people or our ways. Visiting my relatives and dancing at pow-wows with my cousins throughout my childhood likely contributed to some level of understanding. And maybe there was some biological knowing of place as my brother and I sat in the back seat of the car traveling south on Highway 23. *Are we there yet? When will we get there?* It would take our family less than three hours from the farm to my grandma and grandpa's home on the reservation. I can recall the emerging butterflies of excitement when we would make the turn at the stop sign that showed we were three miles from Granite Falls before taking a right turn towards the big open river valley who revealed herself as we drove down the winding hill. It was somehow different from when we traveled to my other grandma's—my German side of the family in Gaylord. True, both places provided an extended loving family. At my grandma Meta's home in Gaylord, we were greeted with oil paintings of an Indian boy and girl displayed in their front window for all to see—perhaps a message to their neighbors or those passing by that they were Indian lovers. Yet going to my mom's side of the family was something special, like a place I was supposed to be. The reservation felt, ironically free and liberating, with room to explore and be. Visits were typically during holidays, summers, or other extended times away from school. My cousins and I would take turns begging my mom to let me stay beyond the usual day trip. Despite her getting irritated, most often she gave in to our persistence.

There seemed to be a deeply rooted desire and pull to be with my relatives in this place at Pejuhutazizi K'api, the place where they dig the yellow medicine. My childhood memories of fun-filled visits connect seasonal experiences to place and land. For example, in the winter, we would climb to the top of the hill where my cousins lived. Then we would slide down the hill past another aunt's house, and finally down to the giant oaks below my grandma and grandpa's place. We would repeat this climb over and over until we could not feel our fingers or one of us was injured. In fact, I hold scars and story to prove it. In the summer, my cousins and I would ride horses, go up and down the deer and people trails, and then bring them to Firefly Creek to quench their thirst –us girls with our feet kicked up along their mane, hoping they wouldn't roll us into the water. We would pester their mom—my summer mother for candy sold at the tribal government building where she worked. We played hide-and-seek and kick ball with the kids on the next hill over and among many more taking turns running around the circle of seated duck duck gray ducks in front of the community hall. We drank spring water from the 'not so secret' spring that was on the side road past one aunt's home to another. During pow-wow time, my cousins and I helped collect entrance dollars from white visitors and pointed to where the secret spring was. It was with my cousins, that as long as we ate our egg and spam sandwiches and were back by the evening—we could be feral children, exploring the hills and valleys along the Minnesota River. It was perhaps due to these liberating experiences with relatives that looked more like me than my Pollack and German neighbors that I felt at home.

I have a lot of these fun memories. Still, it seems I cannot recall any stories that told me about being 'Indian' or 'Sioux'. It seems storytelling was relegated to the adults who were visiting and drinking coffee. Us kids were sent outdoors and to *shut the door or were you born in a barn?* So many of these memories I realize now as I write this, that they are now a part of my story and connect me to my Dakota identity.

During college weekends and summers, I would return to my mother's relatives and land. I longed to be with my cousins, aunties, and family. I would live periodically with an aunt or at my grandma's home during weekends and summer breaks. Finally, upon graduation, I moved there—the pull to relatives, place, and memories being that strong. Today, I cannot imagine being anywhere else. I can remember my grandma telling me, 'Terri, we didn't think you'd come here to stay, we thought you were lost to the white world forever.' This place I call home connects me to a blood line that is sewn into the land. It is where my great great-grandmother and grandfather returned home to after exile, and it is here too where I have continued my blood line.

Some of these stories in this collection connect the dots and fill the voids and gaps of my story. Some provide insight into why things were and perhaps still are. Some stories give me compassion filled understanding to so many things. Most importantly, these stories are significant to me because they tell who I belong to. I am of the people who dig the yellow medicine and the great great-granddaughter of Tasinasusbecawin.

Native Love Jams

Tashia Hart

The following piece is an excerpt from Native Love Jams, *the first volume in the Rainy Bay Romance comedy series, coming 2021. About Native Love Jams: Winnow's latest gig is to forage and cook for a week at Rainy Bay rez's inaugural Indigenous Food Days. A reservation-wide celebration of the local food systems, Indigenous Food Days welcomes guests from Indigenous Nations across the continent. Winnow arrives at Rainy Bay the day after deciding to leave her fiancé Chris, who's out of town with his childhood friend Amy and unaware of her intentions. All she wants is to meet new people, cook, and forget about Chris. As she spends time harvesting wild food with her host Niigaanii over the course of the week, the problems she thought she'd left behind start cropping up and sorting themselves out in unexpected and hilarious ways. While the village of Rainy Bay works out the kinks with its first Indigenous Food Days, Winnow works out the kinks in her love life.*

WINNOW
Winnow turns the jar holding the fist-sized, crusty black and brown, hard-as-rock pieces of birch fungus slowly. Morning sunshine from the window beside her, dances through the cracks between the fungus, commonly known as chaga. The light scatter creates a sparkling kaleidoscope effect on the walls and counters of the nearly

cleared-out kitchen. This sparkle reminds her of the knee-cutting deep snow she had trudged through alone to hatchet the fungus off an old birch tree in the winter past. She smiles, remembering how she had stubbornly insisted on going out that day in twenty below with the wind howling. The smile sours; her fiancé Chris had stayed home to play card games with his friend Amy. They had asked her to join them, but the collective sound of their laughter over the prior few weeks had come to make her skin crawl.

She lets her thoughts of Chris go before they can turn from a simmer to a full boil atop her internally inflamed emotional burner. She focuses on the thrill and joy of the harvest instead; the subzero smell of the red and woody interior of the chaga, suppressed by the cold but still detectable. She sighs deeply and grabs the last piece of brown kraft paper, wraps the jar with it before drawing on a little red heart, signifying the importance of it accompanying her on the next leg of her life's journey.

She grabs another large jar, this one filled with wild rice she harvested with a friend from Leech Lake last ricing season. She opens the lid and takes a deep breath with her eyes closed. She watches the rice grow on the water with anticipation and awe, feels the sunshine and sore muscles from the weeks of harvest, smells the fire and parched rice. Her stomach growls and is followed by a hunger in her heart. Chris had always turned her down when she asked him to be her ricing partner. Not because he was unable to go with her, but because he didn't think there was real value in it if they couldn't make a big profit from the work. She closes the lid and wraps the jar in a kitchen towel. Her cousin Melanie takes it from her, to put next to the chaga in the biggest of all the boxes now occupying the house, labeled 'kitchen.' Most of her personal items are 'kitchen' or 'camping' related.

It will feel so good when all of these beautiful things aren't connected to my bum out memories of Chris anymore Winnow thinks.

Melanie tucks the jar in the box and continues reading aloud the texts on Winnow's phone, "I've always known you love blondes best. Kissy face emoji. Yuck. What a bitch."

"Can you please stop reading that out loud?" The texts have been flying wildly through her mind since the night before when she received them by accident in a group chat between her, Chris and Amy. It wasn't just texts. There were pictures, too.

Melanie shakes her head, her darkly shadowed eyelids enlarge as her eyes squint, "I'm so fucking mad at Chris. He done fucked up beyond all repair, Win. I'm glad you're leaving his ass. You need some joy in your life. I'm so happy we're gonna be roommates. It'll be like when we used to spend our summers together, remember? But now we'll never have to go home—wait, we'll *be* home together!" She squeals in delight, putting the phone face down on the counter.

"Thanks, Mel. What would I do without you? If you weren't coming with me, I don't know if I'd be able to do the Rainy Bay job this week, with everything that's going on." She hands Melanie a clear sack of dried wild bergamot, a gift one of her Indigenous foodie friends had given her last year, gone but for a bit of herb left in the corner.

"You can do anything. I know you can. I've always thought that about you, even when we were kids, you were my hero," Melanie looks at the bag with uncertainty but doesn't ask. If she were to inquire about everything in Winnow's personal effects that she was curious about, they'd be packing well into next week.

A faint smile, "I'm only 2 months older than you."

"A very practical hero, but a hero," Mel gives her a cheeky smile.

Seeing Mel's dimples always makes Winnow feel she's in good company.

Mel tucks the bergamot into the last crevice of available space in the box and closes it up, "There. Last one."

They stand looking at the boxes amounting to Winnow's accumulated 'stuff.' It's not much: enough clothes to fill a small dresser, most things found in a kitchen, some basic catering equipment, and camping gear.

"Just my knife roll left." Winnow walks to the kitchen counter and opens the army-green roll. She plucks her favorite santoku from the magnetic block on the wall. The light from the window gleams off the razor-sharp blade, cutting across the room to land on a half-eaten bag of greasy potato chips. Sitting forlorn and no doubt, stale due to not being closed properly; one of Chris' habits that have always irked her—she gives the chips a death-stare over the edge of the knife, and imagines stabbing the bag, greasy crumbs flying about until they cover every surface. Chris is bad at cleaning. He'd probably be stuck with the grease until he moves out of this place. She smiles.

Winnow is torn from her daydream by her phone chirping like a cricket. She points to the chips with the knife, the chips safe for the moment. She carefully tucks the blade into the knife roll; both of which she had acquired several years prior as gifts from a mentor.

She takes a deep breath and then grabs the phone from Melanie, who had quickly snatched it up and was eyeballing it hard.

It's Amy. *Hey, Winnow. Hey, good morning. Did you get the pictures I sent last night? I see you haven't responded so I was wondering if they went through or not.*

Winnow's eyes narrow, "Is this bitch serious? How much you wanna bet they were drinking last night and just woke up and are now freaking out?"

Her thumbs fly to get out a reply. *I didn't get any pictures. Can you send them again? My phone has been acting up for weeks. Thx!*

It was true that her phone had been acting up, but not in this case. She puts it down and grabs the cleaver off the holder.

SLAM!

Yep, cleaver is sharp, she thinks to herself, hefting on it with both hands to get it unstuck from the wooden cutting board on the counter.

The next message is from Chris. *Morning babe! How was your night? Did you sleep good? I'm not sure what I did to my neck but it's killing me. I might take some Ibuprofen and skip the first session this morning and just chill in my room until I can move it. Love you.*

WHAM!

"I know what you did, you disgusting piece of garbage!" She yells at the phone that's now laying back on the counter, while pulling the cleaver out again and hurling the cutting board across the kitchen. The crockpot shatters in several pieces on the opposite counter, sending the lid crashing to the floor.

She speaks out loud with a phony sweet, mocking tone as she types *Morning babe! I just woke up. Crashed out early last night. I'm sorry you're not feeling well. I'm going to start packing for my trip after I make coffee. Hope you feel better soon.*

Winnow and Melanie stare at the phone. Alas, it lights up again. It's Amy.

I'm sorry I can't send them, I took them with the camera while in messages and they're glitching so I can't open them now. ⊠ No biggie, was just some cool architecture of the city.

Winnow's hands ball into fists. She slumps her upper body over the counter and becomes limp. Then she springs up. She grabs her phone again but this time she scrolls back further in her messages.

She types feverishly, *Has the position been filled?*

A reply comes almost immediately, *Winnow! Good to hear from you! No, it hasn't . . . would it help you decide . . . if I beg?*

Winnow smiles slyly. She knows Jeff has had a thing for her for years. Maybe now's the time to give in a little.

Perhaps ;) How about I come down after my gig up north and you can beg then?

Really?! YES, PLEASE!!! Just let me know when you're on your way. I'll do . . . whatever it takes to bring you on board ;)

She tucks the phone into the pocket of her jeans and smiles, happy with herself.

Her happiness subsides when she meets Melanie's glare.

"Seriously? That guy, Win? You know he's a perv-ball, right?"

"What does it matter if it's Jeff or any other perv that comes next in my future?"

"It matters. If you want to help him get his restaurant going, fine, but do you really think you need all of the extra emotional baggage right now? I know you're like, really mad right now, but come on, not *Jeff*," she says his name with an 'icky' voice.

"Emotional baggage? It could be more like emotional clarity. Just because he'd be giving me some dick doesn't mean I'd have to feel any kind of way about it. Besides, it kind of feels like it could be payback on Chris."

"Ew. You're better than this. Are you seriously gonna disappoint me like this? You gotta let Chris go. Or not, I mean the choice is yours, Win. But either way you gotta let go of that crazy energy I see building in you, because it's only going to get you hurt. Trust me, I know. I've been there."

Winnow takes slow, drawn out strides to the couch. She sits down in front of the laundry basket full of Chris's clean but wrinkled clothes. She remembers. Melanie had been in love in her twenties and a guy had smashed her heart and her car pretty bad. She'd gone wild for a couple years afterwards until getting arrested for disorderly conduct. She decided it was time to change when she saw the look on her dad's face when he picked her up after a long weekend in jail.

Melanie lets her mull over what she had said. She watches her dig into the laundry basket again and again and laughs, "What are you doing?"

Winnow puts the sock she was tying in a knot back down into the basket, "Making busy work for Chris," she looks at the basket now full of knotted items of clothing, "You know what's interesting? With every sock I knotted, the feeling of being emotionally knotted up with Chris got a little looser."

"That's flipping beautiful, Win."

Winnow dumps the contents of the basket behind the couch and flops over the arm of the couch in a full-on droop. She dangles her hands for a minute. She lifts her head, "You're right. I don't want to have anything to do with Chris ever again. I don't want to talk to him, I don't want to think about him, and I sure as hell don't want to see him. Or Amy. Fuck'em," she reaches an arm up to Melanie, whose disappointment has transformed back into her dimpled smile, "Help, please."

Melanie pulls Winnow off of the couch by the hands. She slides over the arm of the couch on her stomach before falling on the floor. She rolls over onto her back, laughing. She lies with eyes closed, "Text him back for me. Tell him, 'Love you.'" She pulls the phone from her pocket and slides it across the floor to Melanie, "I can't do it."

Melanie raises an eyebrow before typing as she's told.

"I don't want him to know I know anything. I want him to come home to an empty house and never see or hear from me again. That's what he deserves. I can't keep forgiving him for shit he totally means to do. I'm like, totally . . . finally . . . ready to do something—somebody—else with my life." She peeks one eye open to look at Melanie.

Melanie shakes her head but can't help but laugh, "And I'm going to help you." She sends the message, "Want me to block his number?"

Winnow gives her a guilty look, "I'm not quite there yet."

"So, what's your plan for when he calls? And keeps texting?"

"I'm going to ignore it."

Mel walks past Winnow and the pile of boxes, satisfied with her answer, and to the stereo that has avoided being smashed as of yet.

The thought of smashing Chris' beloved stereo had crossed Winnow's mind on multiple occasions since receiving the candid photos the night before of Chris and Amy's sexual escapades guised as an 'education conference' in Florida.

"Can we finally laugh at how stupid Chris's taste in music is?" Mel's darkly painted lips lift in a crinkled purse. Her silky, black hair, pinned in a half-up bun, bobs with sass as she tosses her head back and forth. She fixes the strap of her bra, situates her off-the-shoulder black t-shirt, and picks up a cd from a large stack of what could be any number of terrible 90's bands, and fakes barfing. She pulls a bobby pin out of her bun, lifts the lid of the cd case, and scratches at it until she's satisfied. She closes the case and puts it back on the stack.

"It's really, really bad," Winnow can't help but laugh; what else can she do? From within the crushing feeling of betrayal is an emerging sense of freedom. A great opening of space inside her, where a prior tightness, a seriousness surrounding her relationship had occupied her flesh for years. A space where spontaneous laughter now seems to spring forth from. Everything with Chris had seemed like an emergency, and if not that, then there was chaos, and always a lingering, ambient anxiety. Even with the struggle between them, he was always able to laugh. Winnow, not so.

Mel plays the random cd that's already loaded in the player and begins dancing around in as wacky a manner as possible. She is still damn gorgeous, Winnow thinks with a smile. Melanie has always been Winnow's standard of beauty.

Melanie continues to dance, and as Winnow laughs, her body becomes acutely aware how little laughter it has generated. Until today. With the blooming joy of just being around Melanie, she also realizes how absent family has been in her life these last years living in Minneapolis and being away from Red Lake, where she and Melanie grew up. The renewed presence of the essential life nutrients of laughter & family causes her skin to prickle and awaken muscle memory from her youth. "I feel like I haven't laughed—like really laughed—since we were kids."

Mel turns the stereo off and walks over to Winnow and pulls her up to her feet, "We're gonna get you more of that. Pretty soon, you're not gonna remember what it's like not to laugh," She lets go of Winnow and exhales loudly, "It's 9. Johnny will be here soon to help load your stuff. I think we can fit everything in his van."

Winnow looks around slowly, then drops her head backwards, "Ugh. This is some bullshit, Mel." She covers her face with her hands and straightens her head, smoothing her hands down over her face, "I feel like such a fool," she looks at her cousin and can't help but feel better, "but I'm happy we're going to be roommates. Thanks for letting me stay with you, Mel. Love you." She hugs her cousin.

"That asshat Chris is the fool," Melanie says, face buried in Winnow's wavy chocolate hair, "You deserve to be with someone who loves you the way you are—amazing," she pulls her head out, "That includes your smelly feet and kool-aid mustache you've had since you were five, of course."

"I was five! What do you want from me! And how is it on me that you've always had a fascination with smelling people's feet?" Winnow laughs, "All I know is what I don't want to do: stay here any longer than I have to. And I don't know if I'm ready to face Jeff and the restaurant situation yet."

"Fuck it. Let's head up to Rainy Bay early."

"What?"

"Yeah, after Johnny leaves with your shit—it'll take us no time to load—me and you will drive up, check in early, bum around, and just relax for a couple of days before starting the meal prep. I hear they got a good swimming beach."

"What about your stuff for the trip? We need to at least go back to your place and get it."

"I've been packed since," *hiccup!* "yesterday." *Hiccup!* "My bag is already in the car, I didn't know what I was going to find when I got here, honestly," *hiccup!* "Win."

"I swear you hiccup more than anyone I know. Who'll let Johnny into your place?" Winnow realizes she's been so occupied with what Chris has been up to, that she hasn't asked Melanie about the logistics of the move Melanie volunteered to help with.

"My neighbor—*our* neighbor," Mel grins. "I told you about her," Mel adds as she takes a drink, "Rebecca. She works from home, so she's always there and she's cool shit. Johnny's got a mean crush on her so he's happy to help."

Winnow smiles, "Fuck it. Sko!"

"Stoodis!"

"Skoden!"

Ista Wicayaza Wi
"The Moon of Snow Blindness"

Gabrielle Tateyuskanskan

*We had always counted that the year ends when the winter ends,
and a new year begins with the new life in the spring time.*
–Ohiyesa or Charles Eastman

On the northern plains, there are signs the waniyetu or the winter
season is coming to an end. Daylight is increasing, the ice on the
waterways is starting to melt and open up. The snow pack is beginning to thaw and disappear. Huge flocks of geese will soon arrive;
they will fill the sky from horizon to horizon with their joyful calls, as
they announce their return to the North Country from their southern home.

Kunsi Maka, the ancient grandmother, welcomes the reawakening of creation. All the long-awaited signs that *wetu* or the spring
is approaching begin to show themselves. The moods of the earth
can change quickly during this time of year. The temperature can be
warm with the promise of seasonal change and just as rapidly, a late
spring blizzard can appear to blanket the landscape with snow.

The oral narratives of the *Oyate* explain through the Dakota cos-
mology how the earth came into existence. This is an ancient spirit,
one of seven age-old spiritual grandmothers who were among the

first entities from the spiritual realm to assume a physical appearance in the universe. The stories relate how *ehanna* or long ago, *Inyan* or the Rock opened its veins to create the physical form of the earth. A generous sacred gift of a beautiful home for creation to live was given. As a venerated space, it is a necessary commitment for the Dakota to revere and protect our relative *Kunsi Maka or* Grandmother Earth. The narratives further explain how it became the responsibility for human beings to be caretakers of the earth. In this way the land and the people became intimately connected. These are many layered narratives with numerous instructions and moral messages told through the oral tradition. These land- based stories teach Dakota children to understand our place within the environment of Dakota *makoce* or land, the spiritual realm and with other living beings. These essential ideals are communicated through a design with a shape similar to that of an hourglass. The design conveys the meaning that whatever is inexistence in the spiritual realm is to be reflected on *Kunsi Maka*.

These teachings were related to my siblings and me by my devoted grandmothers, their peers and female relatives to the next generation as first teachers of their beloved *takoja*. Through rich storytelling, young people are introduced to the complexity and mystery of *Kunsi Maka*. For *Dakota* children these teachings are a guide to a deep lasting life long relationship with nature. Today there is a serious human-caused crisis in the world. The current relentless pressure for the natural world's resources are having a toxic impact on the earth's ecological systems. The balance Dakota land-based values can provide to protect the environment are a crucial need. Teaching these lifeways could benefit the global community and stop humans from destroying the planet.

The homeland of the *Oyate* or Nation, comprises a vast territory consisting primarily of what is today called eastern Wisconsin, Minnesota, northern Iowa, Nebraska, South Dakota and North Dakota. Including; the Canadian provinces of Ontario, Manitoba and Saskatchewan. The *Isanyati or Dakota* dialect speakers consist of the *Mdewankanton, Wahpekute, Wahpeton and Sisseton* bands. These bands usually occupied the terrain east of the Missouri River and knew this environment intimately. They journeyed the waterways of the Mississippi and Minnesota River watersheds in seasonal patterns. The Dakota followed the ancestral guidance given to the people on how to best use and sustain the beneficial gifts found in the great gardens of the earth. In my youth whenever we traveled with my family to visit relatives, participate in ceremonies, join in sustenance harvesting or social dances, we were made aware of the multifaceted *Dakota* connection to the landscape. This awareness promoted growth in the understanding that Dakota *makoce*, spirituality and cultural lifeways were one.

It is the role of grandmothers as wise elders to be the first teachers in traditional *Dakota* society. The voice of an ancient grandmother, *Kunsi Maka,* in kinship has been continually fulfilling her role by speaking from time immemorial to impart her wisdom to creation. Land-based indigenous knowledge is urgently needed in today's world where human activities are devastating our planet at a rapid pace, to the detriment of all living beings. Our caring relative is committed to teaching her life affirming knowledge of the landscape to guide those who desire to listen and learn. This thoughtful grandmother relates to the first people her story of the earth from *ehanna* in many ways. She reminds the living *Oyate* of their age-old beginnings by way of tangible places on sacred Earth. Many of these revered locations are mirrored above the Earth made visible by the *WicanhpiOyate* or Star Nation through Star Knowledge.

Kunsi Maka reveals her connection as a relative through ceremonies that are specific to venerated places in the physical environment. There are numerous sacred places and ceremonial sites located in various landscapes across the immense territory of the *Oyate*. There are several emergence sites where the oral tradition reinforces and explains how the people came to exist on Earth. In Minnesota, there are two significant origin sites. One location is the confluence of the Minnesota and Mississippi rivers or *Bdote*. In Central Minnesota, another sacred emergence site is Spirit Lake or Mystic Lake. In the Sacred Hills of *He Sapa,* there is another origin site at Wind Cave.

These sites of origin are reminders the people came from sacred earth and are a part of her.

Other important sacred places are the glacial erratic, the Maiden's Rock situated in western Minnesota. The southern point of the Coteau des Prairie, called Buffalo Ridge in southwestern Minnesota, is the place where the pipestone quarry is to be found. Catalanite is the stone that is used to carve the bowls of ceremonial pipes. There are the petroglyphs located in southwestern Minnesota. Thunder Bird Hill is located at the continental divide on the eastern edge of the Lake Traverse Reservation in eastern South Dakota. Bear Butte is in *HeSapa* or the Black Hills. These are just a few of the many significant revered sites located across *Dakota makoce*. The importance of these meaningful sites is related through oral narratives, ceremonies and other cultural practices.

Grandmother Earth teaches the people time-tested land-based values to live by in the present. With the lessons learned from the landscape, there is the possibility to shape a thriving future for the *Oyate*. It was through my knowledgeable grandmothers that my siblings and I were taught to listen to the wisdom found in the voice of *Kunsi Maka.* A necessary guidance in order for human beings to live on shared earth in harmony with all of creation. Through oral narratives, sacred spaces, ceremonies, harvesting activities and observation of the natural world we were taught that all living entities had a spirit and they had a right to existence as members of a nation. The Dakota cultural perspective promotes meaningful relationships between other species and human beings. There are numerous living beings and entities that inhabit *Dakota makoce*. They include some of the following beings: the *Inyan Oyate* or Rock Nations, the Thunder Beings, the Four Winds and the Star *Oyate*. The winged relatives like the insects, bird species and bats. The animal nations with four legs, such as the *Mato Oyate* or Bear Nations, *Sung Manitu Tanka Oyate* or Wolf Nations and *Sunka Wakan Oyate* or Horse Nations are a part of this. The Nations that live in the water; the otter, beaver, muskrat, turtles and fish are included. The many varied species of trees and plant *Oyate* that cover the surface of the earth are also recognized—kinship relationships being vital to providing a structure to live by to promote stability and balance among beings.

The oral narratives demonstrate how the animal and plant nations taught human beings important conservation principles about keeping the balance of life on *Kunsi Maka*. One example is the oral narrative of the Corn Wife. The story tells how the Buffalo marries Corn Woman. They help teach humanity to keep the balance on *Kunsi Maka* by not over hunting or harvesting from the earth. To use responsibly the valuable gifts that she has given to support the well-being of life. All of creation has the right to respectfully live on Grandmother Earth as members of their nations. Each *Oyate* possesses necessary gifts to ensure harmony in the natural world. Human beings are considered a part of nature and are obligated as caretakers of the earth to maintain this balance. This concept is demonstrated by the phrase "*Mitakuye Owasin*" or "All my Relatives." An important phrase that is stated at the end of every prayer.

My grandmothers taught my siblings and me that there are four core-guiding principles in Dakota culture. They are generosity or *Canteyuke*, courage or *Woohitika*, fortitude or *Wowaditake* and wisdom or *Woksape*. These values are reinforced in many ways, including through illustrations in the cultural arts. These ideals are represented in Dakota art by geometric shaped rectangular bar designs. In the traditional Dakota works of art, one bar signifies a core value that is being depicted, two bars meant two values are illustrated, three bars meant three values and four bars would indicate a reference to all four values.

The gift of the use of these designs was given by an elder or a person of stature in the community. At a public event, the exemplary character of the family or individual was noted. Those in attendance would hear the explanation for the gift to the family of the right to use these symbols in their regalia or other accoutrements. In this way, a family or an individual was honored for demonstrating important Dakota values.

The teaching of these land-based values to children promoted the development of an expressive spiritual inner life. Moments of solitude and quiet taught youth to reflect on their observations. Creation had many teachings to impart to young people through interaction with the natural environment. Youth were encouraged to discover the surrounding landscape of *Dakota makoce*. Being familiar with the physical environment allowed necessary connections to be formed to the planet as the geographical manifestation of *Kunsi Maka*. This bond supported self-efficacy through a sense of belonging to place creating a strong *Dakota* identity.

The aesthetic beauty of *Kunsi Maka* was greatly appreciated by my grandmothers. In every season, an aspect of the splendor of Grandmother Earth was often pointed out to their *takoja*. They found joy in the appearance of the first new blossoms of wild flowers in the spring. My grandmothers appreciated the displays of light-ning in an evening thunderstorm during the summer season. They enjoyed the many hues found in the colors of the fall and the crystal beauty of the trees encased in ice or covered with sparkling snow during the winter. It was through their example as children we were encouraged to appreciate and discover the wonder of the beautiful homeland.

The life experience and knowledge of my grandmothers was evi-dent when teaching grandchildren to value nature. They understood the complexity of the Dakota landscape. My grandmothers had vast knowledge of the seasonal patterns and what these signs meant. They also understood the temperament of *Kunsi Maka*. She was alive and to read her moods was important in being prepared to respect her mysterious power. The forces of nature could unleash formidable extreme weather events such as: wind storms, roiling flash floods, pounding hail, fierce blizzards or life-threatening drought. The cul-ture from time immemorial had adapted with humility to meet these strong forces of nature. The people were ready to react and adjust in response to environmental conditions. In this way, the people learned the values of courage and fortitude from interaction with the earth.

The much softer supportive side of the Earth can be seen in the natural environment by her benevolence shown through her bounti-ful gifts. She nurtures and safeguards life by providing necessities for human beings to live. Through her nurturing spirit, she offers food for sustenance, plants for healing, sacred places to guide our spirit, inspiration to create, motivated by the beauty of her spirit and most important a place to live.

Grandmother Earth generously gave the *Oyate* everything they needed to survive and thrive in *Dakota Makoce*. During the spring season *Kunsi Maka* demonstrates her nurturing generosity toward creation. The people learned the value of generosity from the earth. The daylight hours become warmer and the fresh daytime air reaches above freezing. As the spring sun sets, the air can become frigid during the night and nighttime temperatures will then drop to below freezing. Sustenance harvesting of tree sap can begin based on the right environmental conditions. This is the time of year when sugar maples, silver maples and box elder trees can be tapped for their sugar. This activity is labor-intensive and requires the assistance of many family members and friends. Before the harvesting begins, a prayer is said and an offering is given to show gratitude. The prayer would include thanking *Wakan Tanka* or the Creator, *Kunsi Maka* and the trees for their generosity.

My grandmothers enjoyed the cheery atmosphere of group sustenance harvest activities. The Maple sugar camps are happy places where families and friends enjoy visiting and storytelling during the work process. During syrup production, the cooks prepare pleasant meals for the camp harvesters. An elder from the community is invited to say the prayer in appreciation for each meal that is prepared and the sustenance it would provide the harvesters. As a child it seemed the food enjoyed outdoors tasted so much better. There was always a lot of shared work to be done and plenty of relatives who are patient teachers to assist young people to learn the skills of syrup making. The fire keeper must be vigilant to watch the fire in order to keep the large container of syrup boiling at the right temperature. Camp members made sure there is enough wood available for the fire keeper to keep the fire going. The cheerful sounds of activity, smell of wood smoke and the warmth of the fire have always been happy childhood memories.

Maple or box elder trees that are over 10" in diameter are chosen for sap harvesting. The trees that were tapped before in the previous season are examined to find the old harvesting tap. A new hole for the present year is drilled into the tree bark at a different location for the new harvest. This method helps the tree to develop a scar over the wound. The scarring enables the tree to heal itself in a defense against harmful bacteria and stay healthy.

Once the tree has a tap inserted into it, buckets are placed under the tap spouts to collect the sap. Syrup harvesters check and empty the buckets that become full of sap. When the hanging buckets are full, they are then emptied into a much larger container. Then the tree sap is brought to a slow boil over a wood fire. This process evaporates the excess water turning the tree sap into syrup. It takes almost 40 gallons of sap to make one gallon of finished syrup. Each tree depending on the weather conditions produces approximately 3 gallons of sap a day. A tree can produce up to 13 gallons of tree sap during a harvest season. Once the trees begin to leaf or the nighttime temperatures are no longer below freezing the tree saps slows and eventually stops flowing and the harvesting of sugar ends.

Another sign of change in the season is the appearance of life-giving rain that brings renewal to the northern plains. The heavy rains are often accompanied by brilliant flashes of lightning that can occur in early spring thunderstorms. When the *Wakinyan* or Thunder Beings arrive, they send their booming voices rolling across the prairie, the first occurrence notes another sign of the beginning of the *Dakota* year. At the time of the spring equinox members of the *Oyate* take part in a ceremony to welcome back the Thunders. Participants make a spiritual pilgrimage to a beautiful sacred landscape located at the summit of *Hehan Kaga Paha* or Black Elk Peak. This can be a difficult and arduous journey due to weather conditions. During this time of year, *Kunsi Maka* can be unpredictable. The pathways to the top of this peak can be snow covered and icy due to the much colder temperatures common at a higher mountain elevation. It becomes necessary to proceed with caution, making for a very strenuous walk.

It was through ceremonial practices the grandmothers visibly showed their *takoja* by example how the Dakota are spiritually connected to *Kunsi Maka*. Rituals were also a way of reinforcing the valuable spiritual bonds between the ancient earth, other living beings and the Dakota. In this way, our revered ancient connections to Grandmother Earth were strengthened and passed on to a younger generation. From time immemorial, our relative has been guiding the people, teaching the *Oyate* the value of her wisdom. With this knowledge comes a great sense of responsibility to protect the kinship relationship with an ancient grandmother. Respect for her, as a wise teacher and adherence to her guidance will ensure this inheritance for the seventh generation. These ways of being support the valued bonds for young people to develop in the mature knowledge that as relatives they are stewards of a shared earth. Youth then are able to grow with an awareness they belong to and are a part of sacred earth, a vital life sustaining entity, their ancient grandmother, *Kunsi Maka*.

King to Be

Annastacia Cardon

Summary: Hazel Grymes is living in a world with those who have Gifts and has navigated through life with her best friend, Dreagon. He is the one person she trusts, having kept each other alive throughout the years. Suddenly Dreagon has urges to be King and to be the savior of the gifted. Unable to let her best friend wander into the dangers of his dreams, Hazel agrees to help him. She follows him into a world darker, deadlier, and filled with the dead whispering from the shadows.

"I want to be King."

Biting through the greasy chicken leg I shrug playing along, "Can I be your queen?"

Dreagon smiles and the candlelight of the tavern sets his golden hair into a bright halo. "Of course. I'll give you pretty dresses and hundreds, no, thousands of jewels for everyone to see." There's a bright glint in his eyes that he gets whenever he comes up with an idea.

I swallow and take a large chug from my goblet replying jokingly, "I don't like dresses, but I'll gladly take the jewels. And I want a new sword and my own castle."

"Of course!" He grins leaning back and I notice the full plate of untouched chicken in front of him. The long dagger on his hip peeks over the table and the black leathers make his pale complexion striking. He puts his hands on the table as if pointing out a map, "We can start at OreKington. It's a small city with some military supplies so it should be a fine place to start, then we'll head to . . ."

I stop him, "Are you being serious? You're joking with me, right?"

Dreagon raises a golden brow and his sharp sneer is brighter than it should be. "Of course, I'm serious." The confidence in his words makes me narrow my eyes.

Shoving the plate of chicken towards him as I look at my plate covered in bones, "Eat your food before it gets cold."

He pushes the plate aside, "This is no food fit for a king." He snatches my plate away and I suppress a gasp. "Nor is it fit for my queen."

When he reaches for my goblet, I pull out my own dagger in warning, "Don't touch my drink unless you wanna lose a finger." Dragging my plate back to my side of the table I wave for more rum and scratch my dirty scalp. Dreagon watches me. "What's got you thinking about being King?"

He shrugs and I see how his dark grey eyes burn while watching me eat the chicken. "Remember that old man from the village?"

"Which one? The bald one with rotten teeth or the one with the horse?" I say through my food using the back of my hand to wipe away grease.

"The one with a horse." He still doesn't touch his food. He's been acting weird ever since we passed through that village and has been unusually quiet. I thought it was just another one of his fits with the ghosts again. "He said some things while you were in the treasury."

"While you were on lookout?" I question having not heard him tell me he ran into some trouble. My teeth clench at the thought of Dreagon being alone with a stranger.

Seeing my reaction, he quickly smiles and says, "It wasn't bad or anything. Calm down Hazel. He just talked to me."

I drop the chicken leg and lean back. "About?"

Dreagon tilts his head side to side and shrugs, which he only does when he's confused or hesitant. "He-He heard about my . . . abilities." I sit up, eyes wide. "All he really said was how I'm a gift to the world and other crap . . ." He trails off and crosses his arms.

34

"What kinda crap?"

"Well, you know . . . the usual recruitment speech for the gifted and how I could be . . . King." He whispers the last part and drums his fingers against the table. Dreagon always likes to be clean and neat and his fingernails make me conscious of my dirty ones.

I stare at him hard. "No recruitment speech ever says anything about being a King. It's all about joining the army or some body-guard bullshit or a trick to ship you off into slavery. First thing we're doing is getting as far away from here as possible before soldiers start swarming the roads."

"But Hazel . . ."

"But nothing," I snap, turning heads from the other tables. "Just someone knowing what you can do will bring hell on us. We keep moving."

Dreagon slams his fist on the table and the floor beneath us cracks. "I'm done running." I flinch and the candles flicker around us catching even more attention from others. Dreagon glances around and quickly calms downs. The lights return to normal but the large crack under our table remains. "I-We deserve better than this. I can get us better."

I grab his still full goblet. "I like my life the way it is."

"So, sleeping in barns and caves is good enough for you?" The heat in his words sear my skin and I suddenly feel like a wild dirty animal. Hiding how his words affect me I quickly down his goblet letting it spill down my chin.

I smack my lips, "Yes, it is and the sooner you get that crazy King idea out of your head the better."

Dreagon scoffs. "I want so much more for you." He mumbles and my heart stutters.

I reach over the table and take his pale hand in mine. He looks at our hands and intertwines his fingers with mine. "I truly don't need more than this right here." He looks up and I see how my words push deeper than I intend. His hand tightens around mine and he slightly leans forward, but I quickly pull away and drink more rum.

Dreagon pauses and watches me. "I've already made up my mind

Hazel. I'm going to meet Hemlock tonight by the old bridge. He's already made a whole plan for this. I hope you'll come with me."

I choke sputtering rum across the table, "You know his name? It's after a poisonous plant for hell's sake! Can you actually trust him?"

"There is no reason not to." His grey eyes stare into mine.

A new kind of fear blooms in my chest as I look at him. So many questions and fears ring through my mind and I look at Dreagon, my best friend, who is waiting for an answer. I lick my lips, "You know there will be blood if you choose this path. If you're really serious there is no going back."

He nods and massages his palms. "There is blood and death wherever I go Hazel, you know that. But now I want something more and I want you to be a part of it." His eyes plead for me to follow him into this journey and I already know I would follow him to the edge of the world.

I groan rubbing my eyes trying to stomp out the pit in my stomach. "I'm not killing anyone, and I don't want to see anyone die. You need to promise to keep that all away from me."

Dreagon reaches over the table taking both my hands, his eyes bright gazing in mine. "Anything for my queen."

We leave the tavern and walk a mile down the road to an old broken down bridge. I glance at Dreagon along the way wondering if he had planned to be this close to the bridge all along. If his insistence to go off course yesterday saying it was a safer route was purely to keep me in the dark till the last second. I shrink into my coat. The bridge comes into view against the moon's reflection off the water. A cemetery surrounds us on both sides.

I shiver and huddle deeper into my coat. "I'm freezing my balls off!"

"You can't freeze what you don't have." Dreagon chuckles sitting on a gravestone and the moonlight clings to him. He always has some sort of light shining on him.

I huff and look over the cemetery we're in that has gnarly trees randomly spread around us appearing to have sharp claws reaching forward. Most of the gravestones are turning to rubble and the bridge that is now just a pile of rocks sits by a lazy stream three yards away. I kick a stone into the water hearing it ploomph to the bottom. I shiver again and hiss, "I hate the cold."

Dreagon suddenly looks into the dark. "He's here."

"Already!" I breathe and shuffle myself closer to Dreagon in case things get nasty. It's a good thing we're in a graveyard. I squeeze close enough to feel the warmth of his broad back and the unease in my chest grows. He tenses and I see goosebumps line his pale neck.

"He's not alone," Dreagon growls and the ground under my feet quakes.

I put my hand on his arm and hiss at him, "If I fall into a grave like that one time, I'm going to kill you."

Two silhouettes walk pass the graves and through the tall grass in black robes. I put a hand on my dagger concealed in my coat as the two take off their hoods. One has a round grey beard and smooth ageing features; I recognize him from the village. He had bumped into me in the square and apologized profusely. The other is a woman I don't recognize with a bob of brown hair and beady brown eyes. She looks at me and quickly loses interest putting her focus on Dreagon who stands in front of me.

"You said to come alone." Dreagon says menacingly and nods his head towards the woman. "Who is this?"

Hemlock looks at his companion then at me and my spine goes rigid "I saw you brought a friend with you, so why can't I?" His words are smooth as if talking to an old friend.

Dreagon stiffens. "Where I go, she goes."

The dirt under my feet shifts and my teeth clench knowing Dreagon's next move. He's getting ready to hide me in a grave and out of harm's way until everything is safe. Anger and fear rise in my throat at the thought of being stuck underground with a dead guy guarding me. I slowly wrap my fingers around his belt as an anchor, spending the night in the cold ground isn't my plan.

Hemlock opens his palms in surrender. "There is no need to worry, my chosen one. This is my companion, Greena, a gifted child who will help in your conquest towards the throne."

The ground moves more and I see a pair of purple fleshy hands with bits of bone reflecting in the moonlight start to creep out of the dirt next to my feet. I want to scream and wiggle away but fight the urge and try to nonchalantly kick the things back underground. Go away, go away, go away! Two of its fingers snap off and I gag.

"All I see is a threat," Dreagon sneers and reaches for his dagger, as the dead hands grab my ankles quicker than lightning.

I squeak and grab onto Dreagon wanting him to stop. Hemlock puts on a puzzled face and gestures to the space around us, "We mean you no harm Dreagon. Just ask the spirits and they will tell you."

I see him consider this and he whispers under his breath so I can't hear, as a cold wind whips my curly hair around my face. In a split second Dreagon slowly takes his hand off his dagger and the dead hands sink back into the earth.

Hemlock grins like a proud father and Greena, his companion, narrows her eyes. "You are magnificent! Oh, how god has blessed me with the privilege of being your mentor." The old man quickly motions to Dreagon. "Would you like Greena to show her abilities?"

I tense at the thought of her having the first move in anything and nudge Dreagon. Better we have a small army than giving anyone the upper hand. "I will go first."

"Marvelous!" Hemlock grins and folds his hands as if waiting for a treat. I begin to not like the way he smiles.

Dreagon rolls his shoulder and glances at me for reassurance. I keep my hand on my dagger knowing he will be vulnerable for the next few seconds while he concentrates. I nod to him and he closes his eyes and faces his palms towards the ground. I prepare myself for the stench.

Hemlock's eyes shine in wonder as the gravestones shake and the dirt begins to split. I keep my eyes on Greena who watches Dreagon like a hawk with narrow eyes. Then over a dozen different explosions of dirt fly into the air from every grave within twenty feet. The grue-some bodies of the dead begin to crawl back to the surface. The worst part isn't how their rotting bodies pull themselves out of the dirt, or the flesh peeling and rotting off their bones, or how you can see the worms wiggling in their hollow guts. The worst part is their faces, sunken cheeks, lips chewed back showing rotting gums and teeth, unnatural purple and grey of their skin and their eyes. The lifeless eyes that stare right through the world.

Dreagon slumps back with a layer of sweat across his forehead. I quickly look over how many he summoned. Close to forty undead stand around us in unmoving silence. My worry spikes with this many risen. The most Dreagon has ever summoned was twelve and back then he fell asleep for three days with the dead guarding our camp. He must've pushed himself because another gifted is here.

Hemlock claps, breaking the silence. "Magnificent! Just magnificent!"

I wrap my arms protectively around Dreagon as he puts most of his weight on me looking pale and breathing ragged. "H-How many?" He whispers in my ear.

I swallow hard keeping my eyes on the strangers. "At least forty crazy bastard."

He chuckles, "Not so bad for the future King."

"Don't get all big headed now."

Hemlock turns to Greena. "Please." He gestures her forward and we all watch.

Her beady eyes stare us down as she drops her cloak revealing a simple white dress. I slightly unsheathe my dagger pulling Dreagon closer. Greena's eyes turn bright yellow catching the light and she stretches her neck to the sky groaning. She hugs herself close as her body stretches. Scales grow out of her skin and her mouth pulls forward with two long sharp fangs snapping into place. She grows and grows and grows until a rattlesnake the size of a house coils on top of the now shredded dress. Her golden eyes shine, forked tongue flicking and her tail rattles threateningly.

All my hair stands on end and every instinct in my body tells me to run. Hemlock smiles proudly, "She is impressive no? A great ally for our journey ahead."

Dreagon and I stare at the giant snake in equal fear, as the undead army step forward in unison and the snake hisses. The sound vibrates my veins and I feel like a mouse about to be eaten. Hemlock claps his hands and snaps, "Now turn back. We have a long way to travel before sunrise."

She stares us down a second longer and slowly begins to shrink and shrink and shrink until a naked form lays in the grass. Hemlock covers her with the cloak. Though with only the moonlight I can see the grimace of pain on her face as she stands with a scrubbed raw color to her skin. The transformation must be painful and for a second I pity her but then she glares at me and the moment is gone.

The old man holds out his hand to Dreagon. "We must be going now. Our carriage isn't too far."

"Where are we going?" I question and he looks at me as if just remembering I'm still here.

He smiles kindly. "To a safe place for our King to prepare for the journey ahead."

I look quickly at Dreagon, he gives me a loopy exhausted grin and says, "It's all right." So I silently nod believing in him and follow Hemlock out of the graveyard. The army of undead silently follow behind us as Dreagon drifts in and out of consciousness.

We ride through the night and all day avoiding certain roads on account of the undead horde following us at a constant run. Some fall behind losing legs or entire torsos and I cringe at the thought of the poor soul that sees a rotting foot hopping down the road. I try not to look out the window just so I won't see them in the sunlight.

Dreagon is fast asleep on my lap while Hemlock and Greena sit across from us. Everyone is resting except for me and I continuously glance at Greena. She's shorter than me by a couple inches but the muscles lining her body cancels out that factor. I have only caught glimpses of other gifted in the past and having two gifted in the same carriage is unnerving.

There aren't many gifted in the world but the ones that are-are a dangerous bunch. As we move I think of what's to come and what will happen to Dreagon. He's never killed anyone and neither have I and this road he wants to be on will change that very quickly. I'm not dumb to the way the world works, I've been in it and experienced it long enough to know this won't be pretty. Our way of life is to do work for hire and thievery when desperate, we get by on anything we can and whenever things get too dangerous Dreagon summons some undead to scare off the threat. And the farther we go and the more the sun bleeds through the sky I see those days drifting away.

When the sun is setting Greena wakes up and glares out the window, her hands tightly clasped in her lap and a hard set in her jaw. I don't know what she has against Dreagon and I, but I can't stop my body from tensing each time she moves. My hand tightly grips my dagger still hidden beneath my coat and I put a protective hand over Dreagon's chest. My odds against fighting a gifted are incredibly low.

The carriage jumps, sways, and bounces making Hemlock jolt awake. "Oh! We're here."

I don't move and the sounds of Dreagon's gentle breathing fills my ears. I don't want to leave the carriage, but it'll be best to put Dreagon in a bed and maybe these people will be scared enough to keep their distance. Hemlock steps forward and a few people from the group do as well. "We will carry him for you."

I tense at the thought of being separated from him. I promised I would take care of him when he's at his most vulnerable. A sharp whistle splits through my lips and over forty feet march in unison to the carriage. Hemlock and his followers quickly step away and a dead man with half of his face peeling looks through the open door. I try not to look in his eyes and nod towards Dreagon, "Help me move him."

Immediately a dozen hands reach into the carriage smelling of dirt and rot grabbing at Dreagon with fleshy fingers pulling him out the carriage. I hold in my scream when the hands also grab me, I quickly stop my foot from smashing into a dead woman's face. They hold Dreagon and I high in the air and I see Dreagon's head limply swaying back and forth as the dead walk. The smell makes me gag and the unnatural coldness of their skin sends shivers up my spine. Even with all my layers I can still feel the cold from them.

Mewinzha

Evelyn Bellanger

Mewinzha (A long time ago), as a young six-year-old riding in the back seat of my parents' car, looking out the window, I overheard my mom as she said to my dad, 'Mewinzha' and this inspired me to ask, "How long have we been here?"

"Forever," she replied in English. How could that be? I thought as I sat looking out at the young trees growing alongside the road as we drove past. My parents were fluent Ojibwe speakers, and my mom was a Boarding School survivor, a bi-lingual speaker, and practiced oral history. My dad's education was second grade level at a one-room reservation school. She always translated Ojibwe to English for us because we didn't grow up speaking or understanding our language very well. In the Boarding Schools, the children were severely punished for speaking their languages and for not speaking English. This was my mom's and many other native people's way of protecting their children. This would be one of the many encounters I would have on how the effects of intergenerational trauma and the assimilation process affected our lives.

I grew up on the White Earth reservation, an 870,000-acre reservation that was created in an 1867 treaty. This was originally intended to be the only Ojibwe reservation in Minnesota. But other groups of Ojibwe that had settled by treaties in other parts of the state wanted to stay where they were. Only 2,000 Ojibwe would move to this area and settled in different areas on the reservation. The enrolled band members were given land allotments of 80 to 160 acres and the settlers complained that such a small number (2000) of people should not have such a vast amount of land, and the surplus was then given to the settlers. Many loggers and lumber companies soon came, and started cutting the gigantic White Pine, Jack Pine and Norway trees. They cut for about thirty years straight. Today only ten percent of White Earth's land base remains under Indian control. Many of the newcomers would start swindling the land from the enrolled members, profiting from the lumber and land, resulting in fraud and clouded land titles.

The village off the reservation became the town of Ponsford and was soon booming and bustling. It had two hotels, a bank, a car dealership, two gas stations, a grocery store or dry goods, a dance hall, a barber shop, an ice cream parlor, a post office and other small businesses and restaurants.

A few of the businesses were still in operation when I was very young. As kids, we always referred to it as 'uptown.' Some of the memories I had of my interactions with it before it faded and became a ghost town: The gas station had a small garage attached to it where the owner, Mr. Schott did car repairs and owned a big brown Labrador dog that would lay on the counter top. The tall Texaco sign still stands today. The Red Owl grocery store, sold some clothing, and tennis shoes, along with the regular grocery items. The post office was at the forefront of a long wooden building with wooden floors and everyone had a mail box. There was a mansion next to it, with seven bedrooms, a two-story building including a basement where one of our teachers lived and later the postmaster and his wife occupied it. A few others that lived in the area, included our school janitor, Jack Million, his wife and daughter. Someone boasted, 'we had three million people living here,' and that could be true!

Growing up on the reservation side, our community was our world, and as very young children, we had no interest in what the rest of the world looked like. We had and still have many relatives living within walking distance, where we would and still are able to take a shortcut through the woods to see and or visit them all. We bonded as a community and did many events together; Sunday afternoon baseball games, community celebrations, movies, dances and cultural activities. We went through all the good and bad times together and we still have that bond today, except many things have changed.

In the earlier days, the churches played a significant part in our lives. Almost everyone still had tar paper houses with no electricity, and no plumbing. There was the exception of the School, Ministers and Preachers House, the Teachers School Cottages, the Catholic, Episcopal churches and the two Guild Halls that had electricity that were built around the Government School located in the center of the village. This area was always a clean cut, mowed area with tall Norway trees scattered here and there with cemented sidewalks attached to the buildings. The village houses were scattered and nestled in the wooded areas east and west of these along the main thoroughfare that stretches a mile long and on a couple of gravel roads leading to the north and along the one main road south that is connected with the town off the reservation.

Mrs. Peterson, a Baptist, who lived near the government school on the non-reservation side would play one of her 'gospel' songs, every Sunday evening at six o'clock. It could be heard throughout the village. She had a two-story house with a loudspeaker, a bullhorn type that was built into her house, sticking out near the top of the roof. She had an antique record player that she would wind up and play the large 78 RPM records on. Her house would become vacant later and we would not hear her music anymore and the house eventually burned down. I rarely saw her in person—she was a white woman with shorter white curly hair with glasses who always wore dresses and had a friendly smile. I did not personally know of anyone who went to her teachings/preaching or bible studies. Everyone was either Catholic or Episcopalian and she sought followers just as the Mormons did that came around during the summer months. They usually were here for two weeks and would try to convert the young adults into their religion.

The Mormons were young clean-cut college white men, always dressed in black suits with white shirts, black shiny shoes, carrying pamphlets and a bible. They drove a twelve-passenger white van and would stop as we walked along the village road. 'Would you be interested in watching a movie? We also have something to drink with snacks too,' they would say. There were a certain group of us that would hang around together, getting in, we would direct them to where to pick up someone else. The Mormons would hold their little gatherings in a small-town hall, in Ponsford, half-a-mile away, south of the village. It was a small one room building, consisting of many windows with a high ceiling. It had fold-up metal chairs that were placed in a couple of rows, facing a movie screen and a long table to the side that held snacks of chips, crackers and Kool-Aid. I don't remember any of the movies that they showed, I just enjoyed the Kool-Aid and snacks and being in the company of my friends.

One of the young older kids that hung with our group was the minister's son, Melvin. He was a character and comical. He was tall, lanky, always wore jeans and had short, short hair that he didn't comb. He imitated his dad a lot with saying words in Ojibwe that sounded like how his dad would say them. He was kind of the leader in our group and suggested ideas of things to do. "Peck, peck, peck", he would say as he walked down the aisle of the school bus moving his head as if imitating chicken movements as he passed each seat. He had been throwing small rolled up pieces of paper toward the back of the bus. The bus driver saw him in his big rearview mirror, stopped and commanded, 'Pick those up!' We just all laughed.

Melvin was the one who ended our Mormon days. That last day, after we had gathered at their little town hall, we all climbed into the van for a ride home. Melvin was sitting in the back with a couple of his young male friends and he lit up a cigarette. The driver soon smelled the smoke and looked in the rearview mirror and said, 'You can't smoke in the van!'

Melvin said 'What?'

The driver repeated, 'You can't smoke in the van!'

Melvin defiantly took another puff on his cigarette. The driver quickly pulled over to the side of the road, stopped and loudly said, 'You will have to leave the van, because you can't smoke in the van.'

Melvin said, 'Oh, ok,' and climbed out. One after another, we all followed him, all leaving the van and soon our little group was standing on the side of the road. The van quickly drove off and we looked at each other and started laughing. That was the last time we would spend any time or activities with them.

Over by the Episcopal church was the minister's house, and that's where Melvin lived. His family were relatives of our family on my mother's side. One of the village members whose wife was also a relative on my mom's side was the 'town crier' when we had no telephones. He was called by his Ojibwe name, Maa-kee-gaud. He was short, wore khaki pants with suspenders and walked with a limp on his right leg. He would receive notice of someone passing away and he would walk to the Episcopal church and ring the church bell real slow to announce that someone from our community had passed. I remember I was outside and a couple of times I heard that bell ring. That was one of the saddest sounds I would hear and my heart would sink.

My introduction to Christmas was through the Catholic Church where the Catholic community members would come together and gather at the Catholic Guild Hall to receive gifts on Christmas Eve. Just as it was getting dark, my mom and or my grandmother would say, 'get your boots and coat on,' and we would walk the short distance to the church from my grandmother's house. I never knew the significance to what the day was other than we were all happy on the way home and the community came together. The gifts we received largely consisted of long wool socks, gloves, mittens, long knitted scarves, children's books, stuffed animals and a paper lunch bag filled with an apple, orange, peanuts, candy canes, the wavy red and white striped hard candy, old fashioned chocolate crème drops, and small striped green pillow type candies that were different sizes. 'Go sit up front with the other kids,' they would say to me. My mom, grandmother, and other adults sat in the middle on metal chairs and the young men would be standing back by the door. I would sit on the floor with the other kids and look back, checking for my mom and grandmother while observing all the community members in the audience. I would see the elderly women dressed in these long heavy wool coats with fifty cent size buttons. They would almost all have a cotton knitted scarf that was folded in half, as in a triangle form that was tied underneath their chins and they always wore dresses. They would be smiling. The men would have thick wool pants, some with suspenders underneath, a short wool or heavy cotton denim jacket, a cap insulated with fur that had ear flaps and almost all had black rubber boots with fold-over metal fasteners. Soon I would turn back facing the front when the non-Native organizers started to give a little sermon, a little speech and then pass out the gifts, throwing some to reach the far end, making sure to give everyone something.

In our community almost all members either became Catholics or Episcopalians which was decided by the priest and minister in the early days of reservation life. They divided up the members of the community by their church—some of my distant relatives became Episcopalians, and all my immediate and extended family members were Catholic. Since our spiritual practices were banned for years, there were a very few who kept our cultural ceremonies going, Mide lodges were held in the wooded areas. My immediate family members did not practice these ways nor was I exposed to them. It seemed if it was talked about, I would hear about it in negative terms of 'bad medicine' being used. I do remember my grandmother would go off walking in the evenings and saying she was going to a 'prayer meeting.' I asked to go with her once and she said 'no' that I couldn't go. My older sisters and aunts would talk about going to these when they were young. They said community members would go and gather at a persons' house and would sing Hymn songs. Hymn songs are Christian verses that are sung in the Ojibwe language. They would sing late into the nights and have a little food to eat each time. They talked about walking to these different houses and coming home late at night, that it was really dark out and they would carry a lantern for their light. They still practice and sing these songs at wakes.

During two weeks of the summer months, all community children went to catechism, at the Catholic and Episcopal churches located near the school. The Catholic nuns wore the black and white habits, a distinctive feature that remains etched in my memory of those times. In the Catholic church we learned and read the creation bible stories, how to say the prayers of Hail Mary and Our Fathers by memory, and how to do confessions, and take communion. 'You will go to purgatory and burn in hell, if you commit a major sin,' was instilled in me.

"Forgive me Father, for I have sinned, I have told 50 lies," I would say when it was my turn to do confession.

"Do and say ten Hail Mary's and ten Our Fathers," the priest would respond. I would say one prayer each and spend the rest of my time trying to figure out who I lied to, what lie I told and would forget about saying the rest of the prayers. The number of lies would change the next time I went, and I would forget how many I had reported the last time. I never figured out the lies I told. I lied about lying—I learned how to lie.

Every Sunday after completing the course of learning how to do confessions and taking communion, my three older sisters and my two younger ones along with myself would walk the three-quarters of a mile to church. All my family members were faithful and went to church, including my mom and grandmother. My dad did not go, he remained traditional and did not convert to Christianity. He did not write, read or speak English. Most would stop going as they arrived in their teens and a few would continue, and they still have kept their faith today. I would learn that this was part of the assimilation process of our people, to change us to believe in their ways, to believe in their god, and to rid us of our "pagan" ways. There seemed to be rewards given to those who went. One was where we were also able to receive used clothing, free. After church, there would be this non-Native couple that would bring used clothing from the city area and we would be able to go rummage through them at their house. My mom used these old clothes to make blankets. These donations were infested and because of this the community got 'bed bugs.' (Bed bugs originated in two different parts of Europe). To rid ourselves from these bugs, my mom used DDT and would spray this on our mattresses. DDT is a chemical used as a pesticide and was eventually banned forty years ago in the U.S. as it has health effects such as breast and other cancers and it has other long-term effects. We were definitely not being saved!

Summer times were always busy times. I would spend time at my grandmothers' house and watch as she made birch bark birdhouses with my stepfather and they would speak in Ojibwe. I always tried to get myself involved with their work and I would follow her into the woods as she gathered her supplies. Her kitchen table would be surrounded by wiigwass (birch bark), cluttered with bits and pieces, patterns laid out, the wiigwob (Basswood bark) soaking in a water pan while her husband gave her company and punched in the holes with the migoos (awl). She had a regular buyer that would meet with her at a dance where she was a jingle dress dancer on weekends. Her hair was gray with a mixture of black and had natural curls that she kept short and occasionally under a hair net. She wore bifocal glasses and occasionally the dentures she wore made a whistling sound when she spoke. She always dressed in flowered designed dresses with an apron tied on around her waist with light brown long cotton socks that were held up by rubber garters above her knees. She was always in happy spirits and she would make green tea and always offered us a glass, which was in a small mason jar.

She had a huge big garden and I would go help her pick potatoes. She also had a cellar that was underneath the house and the trap door was located beneath her kitchen table. There were some canned goods that were kept down there, although I never saw her do the canning. She would make 'homebrew', in a twenty-gallon crock pot that was kept in the cellar. After making the mixture, with water, malt and other ingredients, it would set for days and then she would take her empty quart and gallon bottles with her as she climbed down the steps to pour and cap the liquor. She would be down there for a couple of hours, and always test tasting her product, we would soon start hearing her singing her Indian songs. We knew it was time to help her back up the steps. She died when I was a teenager, from a heart attack. It was a big loss for me and my heart felt heavy and it was a painful time in my life. I always keep that image of her in my mind and that's the way I want to remember her. Later in my life, I would make the birch bark birdhouses the way I remember her making them.

The Spider and The Rose

Rosetta Peters

My project, a memoir titled The Spider and the Rose, *is a hybrid of prose, poetry, and intimate letters written to my brother posthumously. This story is about love, loss, addiction, identity, and family. This memoir is a weaving of sorts. My little brother, Dean, moved onto the "next place" in the Spring of 2017. I hope by sharing our story it will in some way help others who are out here suffering from the condition of being human. You are not alone.*

CHAPTER 1

The kids and I moved to Minnesota on the fourth of July back in 2011 from Joplin, Missouri. I'm not sure *moved* is the right word. Ran away to or relocated to, maybe. Up until then I had been floundering in a twelve-and-a-half-year abusive relationship with the father of my five children. It was bad. The last time he hit me was on the third of July at a family gathering to celebrate the fourth. We were at his brother Gary's house. All of his brothers and their wives or girlfriends were there, all the kids' cousins, my nieces, and nephews. He hit me in front of everybody. I left him the next day and fled to Minnesota. Fled. That's the word I was looking for.

Looking back, I laugh sometimes when I think of that night. That last sock-to-my-jaw. How it was my personal straw breaking of the proverbial camel's back, the moment I decided to follow through with leaving him. It wasn't the year before, being beaten and stomped on to the point I could barely walk for days, eight and a half months pregnant with our youngest daughter, causing me to spot blood and worry I was having a miscarriage, while our oldest stood in the corner, *'Please daddy don't, you're hurting the baby, stop, please don't kill my mommy.'* Or the morning after, her precious small self, down on her knees beside me, attempting to scrub the bruises off my body, *'Shhhh, momma, it's gonna be okay, he's asleep now, shhhh,'* while I sat there curling into myself, cryin' my self-pity into the bath water. It wasn't any of the morning afters that started out as few and far betweens followed by *I'm sorrys* and *I'll never do that agains*, which became more and more frequent over the years, turning into *why'd you make me do that babes* and *you should've known betters*, but were always, always *you know I love yous.* And it wasn't the nights I had to lock myself in the bathroom to get away from him, or the splintered doors, or the metallic taste of my own blood from busted lips, or the machete held to my throat, *I'll cut you up into little pieces, you stupid bitch, spread your body parts in the field over there. No one will ever find you. You won't even be missed. No one gives-a-fuck about you, not even your own kids, 'cos you're nothing without me. Understand that? You're nothing.* Twelve-and-half years and it was none of that. Nope. It was one quick jaw pop, *don't you dare interrupt me when I'm talking to my brother, you disrespectful bitch! You oughta know your fuckin' place by now.*

My place.

My place?

He was right about one thing, I sure as shit didn't *know my fuckin' place*, but something deep down ya'll, something older than me, an archaic echo buried beneath my upbringing, beneath my childhood traumas, my abandonment issues, self-doubts and insecurities, buried beneath generations of bullshit, something like a song had been growing louder over the years, a humming in my blood and bones and in that moment my entire body and being jarringly agreed, *this is not MY place at all.*

The older two brothers got pissed and made the younger two

brothers take the kid's dad away. *Get him out of here. What you do
in your own home is your business, but that shit doesn't fly here. Rosie,
you and the kids stay here for the night. I'm not letting you go home
with him like this.*

Once things settled down, and the kids were asleep on Gary's living room floor, and I had grown weary of all the, *what are you gonna
do's?* and looks of pretend-surprise concern, I took a bottle of Bacardi,
crossed the field behind Gary's house, and found a tuft of grass to sit
on behind a single bale of hay. That was the first time, I think, staring out at a small pond, with the reflection of the moon and stars
rocking across the water, me gently rocking back and forth with
them, I started prayin'. Hands shaking, taking clumsy shots of liquor
straight from the bottle and whispering between sobs, sweat, and
snot, I *REALLY* prayed with my whole heart. Some call booze "liquid
courage," and I remember feeling like I needed a little extra strength
just then to argue with my God, a Creator I had long since turned my
back on. I mean, this was definitely a tail-between-my-legs moment
we're talkin' about here.

Please. Please, help me. Speaking into the darkness. *I don't know
what to do. I just wanna be happy, to make a home for these kids, I
don't wanna hurt anymore, or be hurt. Please. I know it's been a long
time since we've talked an' maybe I don't deserve your help, but I'm not
really asking for me, 'cos I know that'd be selfish an' all an' I know you
don't answer selfish kinda prayers. Like, I understand why all those
times I asked you to take him in his sleep so I could have peace an' quiet
an' you didn't, that was really selfish of me. I never really thought you'd
actually drown him in his own puke when he passed out like I wanted
you to, an' I know it was wrong for me to hope that. I'm sorry, okay.
And I'm sorry for stayin' with him this long, way too long, an' having all
these kids with a man I don't love. No, I take that back, I'm not sorry
about my babies, 'cos they're the best parts of us both an' I thought I
loved him, I mean, he used to make me laugh, an' I was so young, an' I
guess I just believed, convinced myself, I could love enough for the both
of us, that I could fix him, but I know better now. Shit, I gotta fix my
fuckin' self, an' I know that's not the way it works. But this is serious,*

okay, I'm really lost here. I don't know what to do or where to go but I really need to get the fuck outta here. Have to. I gotta save this family. And I wanna be somebody. Don't you remember? When I was little? It can't be too late for me, I mean, there's so much shit I wanna do. I wanna go to school and do somethin' with myself an' just do more than THIS. And I want a better life for my babies. Even if you decide I'm not worthy of a better life, I promise you they are, they're great kids and they deserve more than this and I'll do whatever it takes, you hear me? I promise I'll make better choices and be the best mom I can be. Look, we both know you weren't really around much when I was little an' you know all the shit that happened an' I've been pissed at you all these years 'cos of it, I mean, what kind of God leaves kids to suffer like that anyway? I can forgive you, okay, I mean, I do forgive you, okay, okay, I'm working on it, forgiveness. I know it wasn't your fault, an' you know I've fucked up a bunch here, too, but I need you to forgive me now, an' help us out just a little bit. I think I can break this cycle. I know I can. This shit stops right here with me. These kids. This generation. I swear, I'll take these babies and leave tomorrow and never come back. I'll do right by them, but I'm gonna need a little fuckin' help from you. 'Cos seriously, man-woman-whatever you are, there's five of them and just one of me an' I don't think I can do this on my own. So please. Please. I need you now. Just give me a sign. Fuckin' somethin,' anything. What do I do? Where do I go from here?

The answer came from the humming in my bones. A tugging. A pull.

Minnesota.

LETTERS TO MY BROTHER
August 2, 2018

Yesterday morning, while I was already crying and emotional from missing you, our mother called. I know you had a hand in that. I feel you in the warmth of her voice. It has been about 3 weeks since I talked to her. Not on purpose, it's just so easy for me to slip back into being too busy. Too busy to answer the phone, too busy to pick up the phone and call . . . too busy to mail her Mother's Day card and gift that have been in my purse for months. Forgive me. I'm not good at this. Feeling. Being her daughter. Acknowledging her as my mother, our mother. I'm not a good person. I have allowed fear to girdle my heart. My love for her has been conditional and unforgiving. Really, I didn't think I had any love for our mother at all. She said, "Rosie, how are you?" "I'm good mom." I lied, not wanting to burden her or bring her down. After all, she's the one who's "mentally ill" and in a nursing home. How could I cry to her, this woman, who gave birth to me, this stranger? The word mom still tastes foreign. Exotic. She said, "I heard a little girl crying on the television and I thought it was you. I could've swore it was you. Sounded like you. Are you sure you haven't been crying?" Again, I lied, "No mom. I haven't been crying." She said, "Last night I read the book you gave me when you came to visit. The one about the little boy in the jungle."

"The Jungle Book? The boy is Mowgli." I said. When I visited our mother, a month after you died, I asked her if she liked to read. I was looking for something to have in common with her. I hadn't seen or spoken to her in over eighteen years. I needed a connection. She said she liked "Little Golden Books." My heart broke to realize that our mother's mind could only process a children's book. I feel guilty for hating her as long as I have.

"Yep. That one. It's my favorite," she said.

"I love that one too, mom, it's one of my favorites."

"Yep. That boy in the jungle. He grew up in the jungle with all the animals. He was raised by wolves. They did the best they could but he needed a village. He needed people that loved him. He needed a safe place."

"Yes mom. It's a good story," I said.

"I was thinking about you, being out in the jungle. Have you found people that love you and a safe place to live?" I started crying. I was feeling in the spaces between her words. "Yes mom. I've finally found a safe place. I live in a village called Marine. Me and the kids are loved."

"Do you have all you need? A kitchen, a bedroom, a bathroom, and a living room?"

"Yes mom. I have all I need. We just moved into a beautiful house."

"Well that makes me happy. I mean that. My Rosie deserves a safe place. I hope I find my safe place someday." I started bawling. She must've heard me. "Why are you crying honey?"

"I don't know, mom. I'm really happy. I am. It's just that I miss Dean. I miss him so much."

"Ohhh sweetie, don't you worry about Dean. He's okay."

"Do you think he's in heaven, mom? Do you think there is a heaven?"

"Why yes! I know it! And I know God would never forsake any of us. Jesus loves me, he loves you, and he loves Deanie Ray. God didn't forsake Dean."

I thought about that. Her "us." What did she mean? Us? We've never been devout. We're not religious. We don't do church. We struggle every day. We try. We have good hearts. It's just buried beneath the rubble of living a life that feels like war. I think she meant "people like us." All the broken-hearted people. Hopeless and hopeful at the same time. And aren't we all broken in some way? I cried more. A sieve of emotion. "I loved him mom. I really loved him." I really wanted to say, I'm sorry. I'm sorry I let your son die. I tried. I tried so hard. I couldn't reach him where he went. Pain took him too far away. I'm so sorry.

She laughed, "You don't have to tell me that! I was there. The minute that boy was born, he was your baby. I ain't never seen love like that. You watched over him and protected him. He was your baby. You two always got along so well. Inseparable. And he loved you too, and he knew you loved him."

That made me laugh. I laughed at her saying we got along so well. What was she talking about, haha, we fought like a couple gun pow-der-fed pit bulls!

She said, "I love hearing you laugh like that. It tickles me."

"What does?"

"When you laugh. Ever since you was little you laughed with all your might. It's my favorite. You should laugh as much as you can. They say that laughter is the best medicine, you ever hear that?"

"Yeah mom, I've heard that."

"Well I believe it's true. Laughing can heal us. And so can food. Good food has healing powers. Say, when you gonna send me that healing stone necklace?"

"I'll send it today mom."

"Good, I need all the help I can get."

I've been thinking about our mom. Her safe place and healing. Her knowing that her mind isn't well. When I visited she said that I brought her peace. That my being there quieted the voices in her head. I think of all the years and fights we got in over her. You urging me to forgive her. *Just go see her, Rose. She's your mother.* Me, stubborn and full of rage, refusing. And it's all so surprising how much I need her now. How I just want her to hug me and tell me everything's going to be okay. How soothing her voice is. How I find the metaphor in her stories. She's not as crazy as they say. How good forgiving her feels. You were so right. And I never listened. I never listened. Well, I'm listening now, little brother.

September 11, 2018

Our mother called eight times. Over and over. I felt panic in her calling, I felt needing. For some reason I didn't answer. Fear, maybe. I don't know. Mike seen that she was calling, he condemned my hesitation, "Aren't you gonna answer it? Your mom wants to talk to you." I thought about the example I was setting. I thought of a future where I was calling him and he didn't answer because he seen me not answering my mother. I called her back. So, I just got off the phone with our mother. She says, "Rosie," her breathing was quick, fervent, "I need your opinion."

"Yes, mom, what is it?"

"What's wrong with me?" That caught me off guard. "What do you mean, mom?"

"They all say something's wrong with me, I want to know YOUR opinion, what do you think's wrong with me?"

"You're mentally ill, schizophrenic. But it's okay. Nothing's wrong with you, mom. I think we're all made differently, special and unique in our own way."

She said, "Demons came to my room last night and said they had my baby boy, and they were keeping him. Do demons have Deanie Ray? I thought he was a butterfly. I thought he got away."

I tried to comfort her, "He is a butterfly mom. I believe that. He's transitioned into something beautiful. The beauty that was always there, that he always had. He's moved into that now, mom. Demons don't have him. I promise. He's safe mom. Your son is safe and happy."

"Are you sure Rosie? It's really scary to see and hear all things I see and hear and not know what's real or not."

"What does your heart tell you?"

She was quiet for a minute, "That Deanie Ray is like that jungle boy, and he's safe now. He's in the man-cub village, and he has a name."

Holy fuck, dude! What kind of twistedness is this? Haha! I feel like you always asked a lot of me when you were alive . . . but this shit . . . c'mon, Dean. What do I even say to that?! She's so fragile. So helpless. I can't imagine what she's going through, in that nursing home, all alone with just her thoughts running through a mind she can't trust. The guilt of all she's done at the hands of her mental illness, gnawing at her. Consuming her reality. I find some beautiful irony in my empathy for her now. How my hate and rage is a deflated balloon the hurt child inside me still attempts to blow up and get in the air, but it's quite useless. All limp and dirty and riddled with holes. I really just want to protect her, despite myself. Who would've thought? And I'd save her now if I could. But these kinds of conversations mess with me. I really don't know if I'm doing anything right here, with her, but I'm trying. For you. For our mother. For myself. I'm really trying.

STAIRWAY
I remember your first guitar,
the first song you learned to play,
Smoke, Smoke on the Water.

I remember Led Zeppelin's Stairway to Heaven
came next. Rose, do you wanna smoke?
I've got some weed, you'd whisper through my bedroom door,
knowing I'd put down my book to get high in your abscess.

With bastard hands and spidered fingers,
you'd play Stairway for me.
I don't remember when the song ended
or when you stopped strumming your homeless strings.

Now, I watch you suffocating beneath
oil and perlite, your teeth
have become ash.
You don't smoke weed anymore,
haven't for a long time.

You knock on my bedroom door,
Rose, I need a ride to South Minneapolis, take me
to Mid Town Global Market.
I don't want to go.

I pretend you're not sick.
At least you're not drinking anymore,
but I don't want to go. I can't stand
the sound of you puking in the bathroom,
to watch you curl into the couch.

On the way, I cry to you
I beg you to stop.
Don't look at me like that, you say,
Don't fucking judge me.
I'm not, I lie, you don't have to do this.
Look at it this way,
I'm giving you something to write about.

I don't want to write you like this,
I don't want to write a poem about addiction.
I don't want to frame you, little brother,
inside that word.

You are so much more.

I've avoided my pen, let it accumulate dust,
because I knew it would bleed your name
and I'd have to carve you into my femur
to keep you close to me.

When we get to the Market
you tell me to walk around,
check it out, grab a bite to eat,
you'll be back in 30 minutes.
Then you leave me.

I pretend you're not sick.

Walking around, I look at jewelry,
I like the hand-made pieces, the art, the clothes.
I cover my face with silk,
and pretend you're not sick.

On the way home you're more yourself,
or at least you want to talk now.
You talk about building fences, buying a truck,
getting back on your feet.
You talk about buying a guitar
and wanting to play again.

I look down at your hands,
your bastard hands,
the ones that just betrayed your body,
held the needle, told the lie.
It was never warm inside her womb.

I wonder if you can ever trust them again
to make something beautiful.

The Sacred Road Trip

Janice Bad Moccasin

Family stories enrich our sense of identity and purpose. A healing journey of many years will yearn for answers in the roots of our identity, family stories contribute to and enrich our sense of who we are and our purpose. It's important to know your roots. I grew up and was raised on the rolling prairies and earth designed creeks of Crow Creek Hunkpati homelands in South Dakota. Our many family road trips to South Dakota were a new beginning to the spirit of relationship to my grandpa, grandmas, the female matriarchal anchors of my lineage.

I felt as if my grandmas heard my prayer cry of "omakiya" help me, I'm having a hard time connecting the past to my present life. I've learned over the years that prayers can be the energy instilled in the heart where the spirit resides. The prayers can serve as the bridge to the stories we raise in our voices of the spirit to our ancestors. I felt as though my family stronghold had been broken and there were missing chapters of resolve, peace and forgiveness. I had never dreamed of the matriarchs in my family nor felt I had a connection to their memorable spirits.

I began to ask my mother to share stories of her life and memories of family growing up in Crow Creek after learning that our Dakota people had been forcibly removed from Minnesota.

The next chapter of my life would be weaving the road trips, driving down memory lane of my grandparents' stories and childhood memories that would awaken my life to dream again—the windshield to open skies of thoughts traveling along with time where memories guide us. For quite some time I felt I had been missing the creativity of my spirit, the inner child.

All I had was childhood memories, and somewhere I had lost the ability to dream, to translate the spiritual direction in my personal ceremonial life. Being spiritually called to share wisdom, offer healing insight, and create a sacred ceremonial space whether in sweat lodge or with the healing horses in the circle for Dakota people and tribal relatives. As well as, a Dakota woman providing spiritual advice and prayer leadership for the grieving families in need of traditional Dakota wake and burials of their loved ones passing to the spirit world.

I did not choose this healing path, I had to learn and immerse my life and spirit in the depth of our spiritual and cultural traditions of our ceremonial lifestyle; first, healing my colonized life of trauma, addiction, rekindling the spirit of my ancestors in my soul; being spiritually open as a hollow eagle bone whistle, through the sacred breath of speaking wisely in a generous heart of love, compassion and truth. Through this spiritual medicine of love, the healer would be transmitted to the grieving families and eventually the blessing would generate throughout the community. I felt truly blessed to generously contribute the gifts that I have acquired through guidance and vision and graciously accepted the spiritual discipline to be an eagle bone whistle.

I have learned to be a helper to my uncle Joe Bad Moccasin who had mentored me in this spiritual role over the years without me realizing that I was assuming a great responsibility. Before his passing he summoned the family to announce that I would conduct and carry the healing forward to our tiospaye. The mileage of many road trips had begun, driving from Shakopee, Minnesota to the Crow Creek Hunkpati in Fort Thompson, SD.

I carried a traveling stone with us in the car as a blessing in my war pony car that would instill memories of our road trip stories. In a special way I prayed with the stone for a safe trip and we carried this stone, an elder from the stars, with us on our travels, sometimes at night. It seemed everything in the car had been in the manner of a ritual, the stone, and sweetgrass medicine on the dashboard. I went as far as even naming my war pony "little blue" who saved our lives a few times. We had all of our spiritual emergencies prepared for our road trips, just in case we had to drive cautiously to watch for deer crossing the roads, and to call our spirits back once we reached our destination after traveling back to the old days that beheld the spirit of who we are as a family. I regarded these road trips as red road drives because I know we found healing in our stories, on this road of memories and traveling through time.

Ceremony is a sacred place to dance, pray and gather to send our voices and energy to the ancestors, to the creator, mother earth and spirit nation. We gathered this good medicine of energy and healing of presence that our people created through prayer. It was our spiritual responsibility to be that message "to live in this manner, so that our life becomes the message." Memories of pain, carried through generations of families and children are in great need of healing and restoring our spirit through these treasured stories. Who knew awakening the spirit of my grandparents stories would spark up my life force energy to be woven into a prayer that I needed to fulfill in my life vision. The sacred stories would reshape my world in my child eyes and adult heart.

When I'm driving down the highway, it's as if my mother could read my thoughts. She began the conversation of grandpa Abel Bad Moccasin who raised me when I was a child. This story of my grandpa Abel made me happy as I remembered my childhood experiences with grandpa.

One of my favorite times is the story of when he would be the first to wake up in the mornings in the house when we were young. He would put firewood in the wood stove to warm it up and throw cedar on top of the stove and it would smell like fresh medicine in our home every morning. He would greet me with his big smile and

smoking his Bull Durham cigarette. We grabbed the metal pails to
fetch water down the hill below at the water well where the families
had access to fresh water. As we approached the well, grandpa would
enjoy the fresh air and roll another cigarette. While I played on the
nearby trees, I watched grandpa become silent while looking at something ahead. I wondered what grandpa was looking at—I saw him
staring at the Missouri River. I followed his view to see many eagles
soaring above the river. I think he was praying. I noticed his forehead, the sun shining on his wrinkled lines of red flesh on his face.
Grandpa Abel was a tall red man who smelled of fresh tobacco, like
an offering of wisdom and humility.·

After his rolled smoke offering, he then would tell me to cup both
of my small hands together to drink the water while he pumped it
before we returned home. As I put my hands together to drink the
water, I felt the cold crisp sparkling water nourishing me as I sipped—
it made me happy. The fresh water tasted cold with a tinge of sweet-
ness and most likely rich with nutrients and minerals. While grandpa
carried both of the pails up the hill, I happily walked beside him. I
enjoyed doing morning chores with my grandpa.

I don't think mom has ever heard this story as I continued driving and taking a sip of my bottled water. Actually this fond memory
brought healing to my childhood and linked me back to grandpa.

• • •

A road trip in February 2020 to Crow Creek would be the greatest
shift in my life, although I would be grieving the loss of my brother
Fabian. He was one of the male protectors in my family, now it is my
honor to take care of his spirit at the wake and funeral services. My
family would be depending on me to conduct the services burial. I
knew I might not be strong enough but I would worry about it later, I
can testify and be assured in faith that everything will work out.

On the last stretch of 20 miles I asked my mom to share stories of
her mother, my grandmother Edith, and great grandmother Sophie
Chief. She began sharing short stories of their lives which saddened

me to learn that grandma Edith had been raised in the residential boarding school. We compared notes of grandma's demeanor, how she didn't talk too much, like something weighed heavy as a burden to her. I figured that she had a very tough upbringing in the residential school. The story that seems to be missing is great grandma Sophie Chief who probably grew up in the stockades in the Crow Creek Dakota imprisonment camp as a child. The pieces of the puzzle begin to build itself against my secret resentment toward both of them for not passing down a memorable grandmother relationship with me as a grandchild. There had been a truth that needed answers to my childhood questions that I may have harbored as a soul wound. My mother began to recount stories of grandma Sophie Chief of how she was stern and feared by our community. This sparked my curiosity about her life and legacy that she left behind with the relatives.

On this journey I would search for the roots of my grandparents' strengths, wisdom, and treasured stories that are so important in my heart, my lineage, and ancestry. I would dream to become the living memorial of the stories of my grandparents, great grandparents and generations past and realizing in my mind and heart that I would be creating and calling out a personal prayer in Dakota traditions, to the matriarchs and grandmas. These thoughts live in my quest for answers to my life.

I prepare myself as we pass the signage of entering the Crow Creek Sioux reservation, our beautiful homelands. There is a great power and mystery of the road down the long hill that we drive toward then opens up to the grand view of the Missouri River and the rolling prairies landscape with endless creeks through the hills, the bountiful willows in the shallow river, sage medicine along with ditches, passing through a few memorial markers where people have passed. As we hit the rough patched up reservation roads that lead us into Crow Creek, the storytelling ends when we slowly drive by the first approach where my grandparents house was years ago. Memories surface up in my thoughts as I drive further in the heart of the reservation.

When we first enter the homelands, we are silent for a part of the drive. I began to think of Granny Sophie Chief known as an old lady who upheld the Dakota traditions in our tiospaye and in our tribal community. Although she was feared by us great grandchildren, and other people on our reservation, she had piercing eyes that could spot trouble a mile away, that you already felt guilty of as she approached you. Those piercing eyes where no lies could ever hide from her because she held the power of her matriarchal foresight. She had such a strong stature about her that I rarely see in these modern times. My mom once told me the stories that would happen at the old post office where the Dakota men folks congregated together dressed in their brown wool slacks, white shirts and dark felt hats. Rolling Bull Durham cigarettes and chatting while their wives went to check the mail. Granny Chief pulls up in her car chauffeured by one of her sons.

As she is getting out of the backseat of the car with her son's help, the men and women would scatter once they spotted her getting out of the car. They hurriedly jumped into their cars and drove away. While she walked toward the door, raising her cane up and shaking it in the air as if she were still scolding them for any wrongdoing she may have heard through keyapi gossip.

We laughed hard about this memory as we arrived at the Lode Star hotel to check and rest for the night. As I rested in bed, I thought about how I had been upset with Granny Chief and my grandmother Edith. My grandparents had to survive the oppression from the separation of family to boarding schools, loss of speaking Dakota language in the home. As more stories unfolded on the road trips, I listen intently as my quiet mother tells me about growing up in our family and how our stronghold became severed by oppression.

Forgiveness unspoken and grieved within my heart toward my mother had been a powerful healing moment when I would cry and forgive her in my heart. There had to be forgiveness in these stories unfolding on our road trips. Ina (mom) had a hard life growing up as a child to a young woman. I am proud to call her Ina, a strong and resilient Dakota woman.

Today I am very proud to be the first family member to attend a university and break the cycle of intergenerational trauma. The intergenerational feelings have been confronted, understood, and transformed. I realized that I have carried this as a burden of trauma with the unwelcoming memories of my family. Knowing my stories hold transformational healing of generations so my grandparents could heal their human spirit of memorable struggle and gather their spirits together to hear our prayers to reconcile the power of our kinship.

The next morning on the day of the funeral, we arrived at the community hall, greeted family and relatives, and prepared for the services. One of my relatives mentioned a Lakota man who stopped by to offer his support. Perfect timing happened when Ivan Looking Horse walked into the doors with his hand drum. I felt very blessed and relieved that he showed up to offer his support, as I whispered "thank you creator." Also, a group of Dakota men carried in their big drum to offer prayer songs for the traditional services.

I looked at our community in the seating areas, their eyes filled with hope as they waited to listen to prayerful compassion and stories of comfort that our loved one Fabian will make his spirit journey home to the star camp (Dakota afterlife). It was comforting that I could depend on Ivan to conduct the traditional services. Ivan instructed me to open with services then he would proceed. I wrapped my Sundance shawl around my waist to bestow strength and courage to open the traditional services. Ivan shared the old ways of our ancestors, the traditions of caring for families during grief and difficult times when losing a family member. He shared the old protocols of staying close to home for a year, instructions to the traditional mourning process. I have to admit this is one of the rare times that I have been one of the grievers sitting in the front row with family.

Finally, Mona entered the building as if I was waiting for her presence. I was comforted knowing she would share a comforting story of Fabian earlier mentioning that she would speak of my great grandmother Sophie Chief who helped her family. I felt as though when Mona walked through the doors, she was not alone, she walked in with spirits who were in our presence. She approached me and Ivan in a respectful manner if she could speak and present the grieving family with a ceremonial gift that she was guided to fulfill.

We accepted graciously. She spoke in Dakota to the people first, then shared her story that enlightened us in remembrance of Fabian Then she requested Ivan to offer a prayer song while she conducted this special ceremony to our family. She then instructed to have the family mourners with supporters behind us to ceremoniously tie the wapaha medicine necklaces around the grievers. I felt moved to cry, wacekiya in a prayerful feeling grateful to her leadership and how she extended great caring for us. This sacred exchange of connection with a beautiful prayer song demonstrated the prayerful deeds to our family which would flourish through the supporters and to their families.

In my heart I felt as though an old ceremony was reviving as she told the story of Granny Chief who conducted this ceremony to her family years ago when her family lost their kunsi. She shared the story of how Granny Chief approached the family and offered the ceremony with her nieces who cooked the feast food for the family. Granny Chief had made the same medicine pouches for the family and conducted this ceremony at their Kunsi's funeral services.

My heart opened like thunder letting in the love of my great Granny Chief! I thought granny you have come to help us through this Dakota winyan whose lives you have touched now this healing ceremony has returned to our family! I fell to my knees in humble awakenings and tears of humility as my soul released the anger with Granny Chief and grandma Edith. The healing surges in every fiber of hidden haunts in my body and spirit, these moments were shifting me through a portal of healing with great presence of spirit. My spirit nudged me and told me that my Granny Chief and her daughter Edith who walked in those doors in spirit with Mona to speak to our family and community.

The rest of the night was filled with traditional prayers, songs, aroma of medicines, comforting times for the people. Listening to stories, kindness extended to the supporters, the younger kids fetching coffee for the older folks. After closing out services, the relatives and family had served the meal to feed the people. Before I left to retire for the night, I visited with old friends, catching up with my relatives in laughter, a way to ease the sadness.

I have never been so happy in my life to witness the returning of a loved ones' spirit in this sacred manner. This story had a spirit attached to it in our road travel conversations, it was all coming together. After the burial and feast, we were already packed up for our long drive back to Minnesota. It was a quiet and peaceful drive all the way home. In my vision of thoughts while driving and being the only one awake, I cried tears of joy to my grandpa Abel for keeping the story alive with me, grandma Edith for her sacrifice to survive and carry our family until she could no longer, and Granny Chief for being so strong and prayerful, lastly gifting our family her ceremony for the grieving, nina pidamaya, such immeasurable thanks. I was driving home with the greatest blessing of having peace in my spiritual responsibilities and I had our matriarchs' blessing to continue the walk of life in their honor. Today I can hear the eagle bone whistles in my spirit, memories of grandpa praying to the eagles in his quiet powerful offerings. The blessings I received is in the power of my will and determination to give back as a wopida, immeasurable thanksgiving that would be "living in a manner, that your life becomes the message."

Naming Ceremony

Zibiquah Denny

DRUM DANCE

Drum dance time! Every spring and fall my family of two brothers, two sisters, mom and me, would climb into Uncle Tommy's car and ride for three hours north to Wisconsin Rapids from our home town of Milwaukee, Wisconsin. Since we were kids, sitting still in a cramped car for three hours was torture but once we got there we knew we would have to sit still for two more days in the dance ring. Hmm, three hours compared to eight hours, this part of the journey was the easy part.

If we acted up, mom's look or her suddenly long arm with a fist at the end of it would be the only thing we needed to see or feel before we all shut the hell up. Mom was the boss and she let us know it. The only thing that we liked about these trips was that we got to see our grandparents. This time, however, was even more special for me, I was getting named this year and I was excited.

We stayed with our grandparents, Thomas (Misho) and Dora (Goko) Kitchkume, two of the sweetest elders in the world. Big smiles, hugs and kisses always greeted us when we got to their small but loving home. Their two-bedroom house was a nine-hundred foot A frame with a gravel driveway. I remember their pine cabinetry in the kitchen was homey and something was always cooking. Goko would always have food and snacks for us. I loved her corn and hot dog soup. YUM!

My mom's younger sister, Aunt Ramona or Auntie Mona as we called her, drove in from the west. A quiet but powerful presence, she was usually there when we pulled in. Auntie Mona lived in Onalaska which was about an hour west of Rapids. The two sisters were so close, they even used to write letters to each other, which I thought was cute. She always had gifts for us kids—so generous and sweet. I admired her a bunch.

The sleeping arrangements went like this:

Auntie Mona slept on a cot in the kitchen and mom and us kids would make a big bed on the living room floor.

Misho would sleep in the bigger bedroom and Goko in the smaller room. Uncle Tommy would sleep in Misho's room. I would hear them talking well into the night. Uncle Tommy was a World War II veteran. He fought in the Philippines and when he came back he never talked about that experience. He did tell Misho that when all of his buddies hit the beach and everyone was getting killed around him, he heard the drum.

Uncle Tommy never missed a Drum Dance after that. Sometimes mom would call him a fanatic, but that was just brother and sister banter. We would never disrespect him or dare talk back to him. Except one time when me and my brother Jack were throwing the football in the yard at my Grandparents' house and he came out and told us we were not supposed to play during the Drum Dance. I pretended not to hear him but when he demanded the football, I threw it at him, the way my bro taught me, straight shot with a spiral. It hit him between the stomach and the chest and then fell to the ground— he quickly picked it up and stalked in the house.

Later my brother Jack said with a smirk on his face, "Geez Ruthie, why did you throw that football at Uncle Tommy like that?"

"Because I was mad, why does he have to ruin our fun all the time? We weren't bothering anybody." We both burst out laughing.

"You're lucky mom didn't see you."

"I told her about it. Mom and Auntie Mona thought he went too far. Mom was kinda mad herself. What were we supposed to do, sit

around and get in the way of everybody cooking and getting ready?"
Mom never confronted her little bro Tommy about snatching up our
football. They had more important things to talk about I'm sure.

Uncle Tommy always had a military style crew cut which meant
no more than one inch of hair anywhere on his head. One time my
cousin Larry asked him, "Hey Tommy, when you gonna get a haircut?"

As we all tried not to laugh, Tommy's reply was, "Heh, heh, heh!"

There was no one like Uncle Tommy, he was so one-track minded.
Unfortunately he never had any children which was such a shame.
He was married to an older Menominee woman who could not have
children. My grandfather was not happy about Tommy not having
children. He told Tommy, "The name Kitchkume ends with you."
Powerful words and a harsh reality we all felt. Uncle Tommy had no
one to carry on his name or the teachings that were so important in
our lives as Potawatomi people.

He knew everything about the Drum Dance and he always danced
hard in the ring even when his arthritis kicked in. He was an honored
teacher and taught all the young guys what they needed to know—
their duties, their songs, and their responsibilities in order to keep the
Drum Dance going. He wore the same kind of blue jeans and flannel
shirt with old overturned moccasin type shoes. He always looked
so pitiful. My mom used to buy him new clothes for his birthday
and Christmas but he never wore those things and my mom used to
wonder why. Well we never found out but that was Uncle Tommy—
he never liked change. He was highly respected by all and nobody
wanted to be yelled at by him. And that's what he did, he kept the
drunks and the white people out of our Drum Dance and kept all of
us kids in line. Nobody wanted to be yelled at by Tommy.

At five o'clock in the morning when it was still dark outside, Uncle
Tommy would get up and say in his loud voice, "Rise and Shine!"

SKUNK HILL

The Potawatomi originally lived along Lake Michigan from Indiana,
to Illinois to Green Bay, Wisconsin. Over 300 miles of villages and
encampments were formed around Lake Michigan.

In 1830 Congress passed the Indian Removal Act and President Andrew Jackson signed into law the plan to relocate all Native people living east of the Mississippi River to a designated Indian territory in the states of Nebraska, Oklahoma, and Kansas to be held in trust by the US government. The Treaty of Chicago signed in 1833 forced the Potawatomi off Lake Michigan onto lands in Iowa and Kansas, where the Prairie Band Potawatomi Reservation was started.

We went from Lake front property owners on Lake Michigan to living in a lifeless dustbowl without good soil to grow crops, no trees and no big lakes.

When the soldiers came to remove the Potawatomis, some resisted and escaped into the woods of Northern Wisconsin and Canada while some lived as virtual refugees on their former lands. My great-great-grandfather was part of this removal. They soon realized that living on the reservation was no life. They were constantly watched by the soldiers and the missionaries moved in to Christianize them all. The Potawatomis were not allowed to practice their religion, speak their language or live the way their ancestors had for thousands of years. Fed up with reservation life and being virtual prisoners on their own land, by the 1860's several hundred started moving back to their homelands in Wisconsin.

In 1887 the Dawes Allotment Act went into effect. It was designed to get rid of the reservations—make farmers and landowners of Natives. The Act carved the communally-owned reservations into individual holdings called allotments, that were given to enrolled members of the reservation along with the ability to sell or lease their land to white farmers. Many of the enrollees did so because they had no other income.

Millions of acres of Native owned land were lost forever.

Some Native people saw the writing on the wall, including a small group of Potawatomi people in Kansas who used that lease money to buy land where they could practice their religion in peace. My great-grandfather, Thomas Kitchkume and his wife, Nom-kom-go-quah and their children were part of these movements. My grandfather or Misho, a full-blood Potawatomi was born on the reservation in Mayetta, Kansas but grew up in Wisconsin. Both named Thomas Kitchkume, my great-grandfather raised his family in Wisconsin. In 1905, they eventually found a place on a hill in central Wisconsin near a large quartzite rock that resisted the glaciers that flattened the surrounding landscape. Here they quietly resisted the forces that tried to crush their culture and loudly practiced what would become a seasonal dance with the drum at the heart of these ceremonies—this place was called Skunk Hill and the ceremony was called the Drum Dance.

My Uncle Tommy told us the story of how some of his relatives had visions of a place on a hill in Wisconsin that was all lit up. The spirits were calling them and they needed to move to that place. They would call that place Skunk Hill or Tah-qua-kik.

In the late 1870's a young Lakota girl, named Tail Feather Woman had visions of a big drum with ceremonies surrounding it. She shared her dream in the hope that the drum would help Native people live in peace and survive the onslaught of violence, fear and hatred surrounding them. This vision was shared by Native people living in the Dakotas, Minnesota, Wisconsin and Michigan—these dances would be known as the Drum Dance or the Big Drum ceremonies. They would become a sanctuary for Native people all over the upper Midwest. Many people from Kansas and Iowa would travel to participate in these four-day-long ceremonies.

Many openly travelled back and forth between Kansas and Wisconsin and became absentee members of the Prairie Band Potawatomi. The authorities found out about the escapees and tried to bring them back to Kansas, but discovered it was useless because they would always find their way back to Wisconsin. Although the ceremonies were forbidden, Indian agents felt reluctant to interfere with them. The agents viewed the Wisconsin Potawatomi as "troublesome and insubordinate" because of their opposition to allotments as well as their promotions of Native traditions.

NAMING CEREMONY
The spring of 1968 and I am ten years old—I was excited for the spring dance to start. With spring time came reawakening and renewal

when new members would be initiated and Potawatomi names given out. This was the year I was going to be given a name by my grandfather at the Drum. It was a big deal. Mom said that there would be a song, a speech, a feast and a name—all in Potawatomi. My family would provide the feast. Days before my mom and I went shopping for a new dress and new shoes. I picked out a blue flowered dress with a white top and a matching jacket. The shoes were black shiny patent leather. I felt like Cinderella going to the ball without the mice or carriage but with my Uncle Tommy's big cramped and crowded Ford.

Mom's instructions: "Mike, my brother (who was a singer on the Drum) will come get you and walk you to Misho who will speak for you, stand by him until he is done. He will send you back to sit down, and then there will be a song. After that, some people will come over to shake your hand, give you money or gifts and you will say, 'Migwetch.' Nothing to worry about."

"Okay mom." I was getting anxious now. I did not know I would have to stand in front of everybody.

Mom must have seen the look on my face and she said, "Ruthie don't worry it will go faster than it sounds and everyone will be happy for you."

Auntie Mona, my mom and my sister Joyce cooked up a storm that day. We loaded up the cars with the food and headed to the ceremony. All eyes were on me that day. I stood tall and proud next to my grandfather who was highly respected by everyone. The name I was given that day was Zibiquah, which means River Woman.

After the speech, songs and gifts, we got to feast on frybread, corn soup, hominy soup, beef and barley soup, wild rice dishes, pasta dishes, cakes, pies, green tea and juice.

I carry that name proudly to this day and hold that memory with love, beauty and honor. What baffled me was that I was not allowed to tell anyone about what transpired on my special day or anything about these ceremonies. Mom sternly instructed me, "Ruthie you can't tell anyone about these dances. Don't ever tell anyone outside the family about them you hear?" My mom and uncle were very serious, I got the message but I still didn't get it. No explanation was ever given to me, I asked my siblings and they never told me anything either. I was in bad need of some satisfaction and some answers. I was befuddled, perplexed.

I wanted to tell my friends at school, I wanted to share my experience and get some feedback on the coolness of the whole thing. So my rebellious mind which is in my DNA by the way, made me disobey and I told my best friend Teresa who was a red-haired-freckled face white girl who I trusted and was a good listener. She thought it was so cool and said she wished she could get a new name. Even though I told Teresa not to tell a soul, I started to feel guilty and scared after I told her—I thought I was going to be struck down by lightning or something but nothing happened which only made me more confused. I never told anyone else.

I finally got my answer when I attended the University and took a Native American history class. As a result of the harsh assimilation policies which lasted through the 1880's to the 1930's which made Native religion and language illegal—many Native people were shot down by the military or sent to prison for practicing their traditional religious ceremonies. Drum Dance and all other traditional Native ceremonies went underground and were held in secret. No show, no tell, how do you explain that to your ten year old child?

RELIGIOUS FREEDOM
I get it now. We are supposed to be happy because they removed my people from our beloved and beautiful Lake Michigan, our ancestral homelands and placed us on a lifeless dustbowl, then slowly started chipping away at the reservation while the military and the missionaries robbed us of our language, our religion, our culture and eventually even our children. The reservations were nothing but concentration camps and my ancestors were the prisoners. In a country that was formed because of the lack of religious freedom in Europe—they outlawed the religion of the original inhabitants—the irony.

My great-grandfather was an escapee, a revolutionary—an insubordinate.

Unfortunately, the community of Skunk Hill dissolved in the 1930's mainly for economic reasons. Some families moved nearby, some joined the military and some moved away to the cities to find work. Soon after the last Potawatomi family left Skunk Hill, the land became a park called Powers Bluff. The two tree lined dance rings and the cemetery have become a Wisconsin State Historical site. Sometimes we go there to put down seyma and pray. A book was written about the history and the descendents involved in the battle to make Powers Bluff an historical site in order to preserve the rings and keep the cemetery intact.*

In 1978, Congress passed and President Jimmy Carter signed the American Indian Religious Freedom Act which states, "It shall be the policy of the U.S. to protect and preserve for American Indians their inherent right of freedom to believe, express and exercise the traditional religions . . ."

The Drum Dance continues to this day on private property owned by the descendents of Skunk Hill. We no longer have to worry about being arrested or killed for praying and giving thanks to the earth, to the animals, to our ancestors or for naming our children by the drum. Some members still believe we have to keep it all on the down low. I am not of that mindset. I think the world needs to know.

From sitting for hours as a child I learned perseverance, patience and respect. I learned the power of prayer, food, family and the strength in communal prayer, feast, song, dance and the drumbeat, the heart beat of the people and the planet. I learned we are connected not only to each other but to the earth.

I still attend these dances though they have changed—our elders are gone, our language has changed from Potawatomi to English, some of the songs and ceremonies that go together have been lost. The beauty of the songs is still there, but I yearn for the days of hearing my elders make long speeches in Potawatomi; Getting told by my mom to "Sit Still!" Hearing my grandfather, my grandmother, my mom, my aunties, my uncles, my sisters and brothers' sing and

---

* Skunk Hill, A Native Ceremonial Community in Wisconsin, by Robert A. Birmingham; The State Historical Society of Wisconsin, 2015.

pray; Being part of those special people singing, dancing and praying together. The messages of thanks and love in those ceremonies will never leave me.

I am blessed to have ancestors who had visions and wanted their future generations to have the knowledge and wisdom of their way of life—their way of giving thanks to all life on this earth. I am blessed that they were stubborn, insubordinate and troublesome.

I am Zibiquah.

Contributors

Photo: Ne-Dah-Ness Greene

Janice Bad Moccasin is a Dakota/ Lakota Spiritual Advisor who has shared ceremonial based healing work with individuals, families and communities who have been impacted by trauma. She is a visionary thinker, eloquent speaker and has been writing a collection called Java Reflections on social media for the past six years and has empowered an audience. Janice is part of the Native American Women's Writing Cohort. She is writing a memoir which takes you on a journey of transforming trauma to awakening an inner voice of freedom who carries forward her ancestor's resilience, teachings, and personal ceremonial healing.

Evelyn Bellanger lives at and is an enrolled member of the White Earth Ojibwe Nation. She is an environmental activist and has actively supported stopping DAPL (Standing Rock), Stop Line 3 (Palisade, MN) and is a member of The Rights of Manoomin (Wild Rice) Committee. She is a member of White Earth Elders Indian Affairs Commission, and publishes articles in the White Earth tribal newspaper, *Anishinaabeg Today*. She is currently working on a memoir of living on the reservation and how historical trauma touched her life. She has a masters' degree in American Indian Studies.

Photo: Evelyn Bellanger

Annastacia Cardon is an Ojibwe woman enrolled in Leech Lake. She is eighteen years old, began writing at thirteen, and published a poem in *Yellow Medicine Review* 2020. Her writing ranges from poetry to creative fiction. She is currently working on a fantasy novel for publication. Passionate hobbies include beekeeping, dancing, and being an active member in the Minneapolis Native community. She recently completed her freshman year in college.

Photo: Ne-Dah-Ness Greene

Photo: Ne-Dah-Ness Greene

Zibiquah Denny is Potawatomi (People of the Fire) and Ho-Chunk (People of the Sacred Voice) originally from the great lakes and woodlands of Wisconsin. She is a storyteller—telling stories that educate, preserve history and culture and hopefully inspires. Former editor of *The Circle* newspaper and Executive Director of the Native American Journalists Association, she recently guest edited the *Yellow Medicine Review*, Spring 2020 issue. *Water-Stone Review* is publishing her essay called, "The Buckskin Dress" for the fall 2021 issue. Ruth is currently writing a memoir.

Photo: Ne-Dah-Ness Greene

Tashia Hart (Red Lake Anishinaabe) is an award-winning author and illustrator of *Gidjie and the Wolves* (Not Too Far Removed Press, 2020) and *Girl Unreserved* (2015). Forthcoming works include: a cookbook, The Good Berry: Harvesting and Preparing Wild Rice and Other Wild Foods (Minnesota Historical Society Press 2021); Native Love Jams, a romantic comedy; and a comic book, *Kid Epicurious*. She's the illustrator of three books in the *Minnesota Native American Lives Series* (Wise Ink Creative Publishing, 2020), and her short works include recipes/essays for PBS, First Nations Development Institute and others.

Rosetta Peters is a poet, an author, a public speaker, and an activist. She is of Yankton, Crow Creek, and Oglala descent. A procrastinator to the point of detriment and lover of the natural world, Rosetta has had her poetry published in the *Yellow Medicine Review* and has recently been awarded the Minnesota State Arts Board Artist Initiative Grant 2021 to professionally record and release an album of her Spoken Word/Performance Poetry and the MRAC Next Step Grant 2021/2022 for creative support for the completion of her memoir titled, The Spider and The Rose."

Photo: Ne-Dah-Ness Greene

Teresa Peterson, UtuhuCistinna Win, is Sisseton Wahpeton Dakota and member of the Upper Sioux Community. She is the author of Grasshopper Girl, a children's book published by Black Bears and Blueberries Publishing. Her poetry has appeared in "The Racism Issue" of the *Yellow Medicine Review*. Teresa and her uncle, Super LaBatte, co-wrote their forthcoming book, Voices from Pejuhutazizi: Dakota Stories and Storytellers, Minnesota Historical Society Press, that will be out late 2021. Her true passion is digging in her garden that overlooks the MniSota River valley and feeding friends and family.

Photo: Ne-Dah-Ness Greene

Photo: Ne-Dah-Ness Greene

Gabrielle Wynde Tateyuskanskan lives in the rural community of Enemy Swim on the Lake Traverse Reservation in South Dakota. She is a visual artist, writer and poet. Gabrielle is a long-time member of the Oak Lake Writers. Her work has been published in *The American Indian Quarterly, The Footsteps of Our Ancestors: The Dakota Commemorative Marches of the 21st Century, This Stretch of the River, HeSapa Woihanble: Black Hills Dream, Beloved Child: A Dakota Way of Life, What Makes a South Dakotan* and *The Yellow Medicine Review.*

Photo: Sarah Whiting

Diane Wilson, a Dakota writer, has recently published a new novel, The Seed Keeper, by Milkweed Editions. Her memoir, Spirit Car: Journey to a Dakota Past, won a 2006 Minnesota Book Award and was selected for the 2012 One Minneapolis One Read program. Her nonfiction book, Beloved Child: A Dakota Way of Life, received the Barbara Sudler Award from History Colorado. She has received numerous grants, including a 2013 Bush Fellowship, and the 2018 AARP/Pollen 50 Over 50 Community Leadership award. Wilson is enrolled on the Rosebud Reservation and serves as Executive Director for the Native American Food Sovereignty Alliance.

Acknowledgements

The Native Authors Program was created through a partnership between All My Relations Arts, an initiative of the Native American Community Development Institute, and the Hennepin County Library.

All My Relations Arts (AMRA) operates the All My Relations Gallery, Minnesota's premier American Indian owned and operated contemporary fine arts gallery. Located on Franklin Avenue in Minneapolis, the gallery resides within the heart of the American Indian Cultural Corridor. AMRA presents four fine art exhibits throughout  the year, as well as hosting tours, presentations, and programs. As an initiative of the Native American Community Development Institute (NACDI), the focus of AMRA is to provide the people of the Twin Cities, greater Minnesota, and beyond consistently high-quality exposure to Native American fine arts. Learn more about All My Relations Arts at allmyrelationsarts.com

Native American Community Development Institute (NACDI) Our work is founded on the belief that all American Indian people have a place, purpose and a future *strengthened* by

sustainable community development. NACDI initiates projects that benefit the Native community, often in partnership with other Indigenous-led organizations. Our future is bright due to the resilience and vision of our ancestors. Founded in 2007, NACDI is approaching its second decade with a renewed commitment to the Indigenous values that helped our people persevere despite centuries of hardship. Learn more about NACDI at nacdi.org.

Hennepin County Library is one of the nation's largest public library systems, serving 1.2 million residents across 611 square miles. With 41 locations and robust online services, we connect rural, urban, and suburban communities with innovative library services. We nourish minds, transform lives, and build community together. Our digital and physical collections seek to preserve the past, inform the present, and inspire the future.

HENNEPIN COUNTY
LIBRARY

We would like to give special thanks to **Juli Bratvold**, the graphic designer for Hennepin County Library.

Layout, design and printing of this anthology was provided by **Blacks Bear and Blueberries**, a Native owned non-profit publishing company, with a focus on creating and developing Native children's books for all young people written by Native authors and illustrators.

The Native Authors Program was funded in part by **Minnesota's Arts and Cultural Heritage Fund**.  Minnesota Humanities Center  CLEAN WATER LAND & LEGACY AMENDMENT